The Ghost in the Hollows

PATRICIA KOMAR

ARCHWAY
PUBLISHING

Archway Publishing books may be ordered through booksellers or by contacting:

Archway Publishing
1663 Liberty Drive
Bloomington, IN 47403
www.archwaypublishing.com
1-(888)-242-5904

ISBN: 978-1-4808-0825-6 (sc)
ISBN: 978-1-4808-0827-0 (hc)
ISBN: 978-1-4808-0826-3 (e)

Library of Congress Control Number: 2014911737

Printed in the United States of America.

Archway Publishing rev. date: 07/14/2014

CHAPTER 1

Electrifying!

ZZZZAAAAAPPP!

Faith Clancy followed her mother up the walkway to Hollow Hills Middle School. She took her first step through the large green front door. Without any warning, a bolt of lightning zapped through her body. A splash of neon rainbow colors blinded her. Seconds later it was gone. At that precise moment she knew. Yes, she knew this was not just another middle school. There was something mysterious and electrifying happening here.

Faith stood frozen like an ice statue just inside the doorway. She looked left and then right. Mrs. Clancy, Faith's mother, totally oblivious to what had just happened, turned right and continued through the next door, a beige door with big turquoise letters that said Office. Obviously Mrs. Clancy hadn't felt a thing. Whatever had just happened was felt and seen by Faith and Faith alone. This was just the beginning. Faith shook it off, like a dog after coming out of a bath. She followed her mom through the beige door and into the office.

"Can I help you?" a voice coming from out of nowhere squeaked.

Faith looked around. She didn't see anyone.

Then slowly edging up, a face peered from behind the counter. The voice said again, "Can I help you?" A copper-colored name-plate sitting on the counter next to a vase of orange and yellow flowers announced to the world the voice belonged to Ms. Cooper, Secretary. "Hellooo, can I help you?" Ms. Cooper squeaked again as she stretched higher and higher trying to be seen.

Mrs. Clancy replied, "Oh, there you are. I'm here to register my daughter for school."

Ms. Cooper's head sank below the counter. There was a tick, tick, tick of phone buttons. "Miss Flemings, you have a new student." Her head popped up this time. "Please have a seat. The counselor, Miss Flemings will be with you momentarily."

Faith heard the click, click, click of footsteps approaching them. A young lady with long, straight black hair wearing a fuchsia lace top over black slacks appeared and extended her right hand. "Hello, I'm Miss Flemings. And you are?"

"I'm Andrea Clancy," she said, shaking the counselor's hand, "and this is my daughter, Faith."

"Welcome to Hollow Hills Middle School. Please follow me," the counselor directed.

They walked down a long, narrow hallway. Faith noticed how the counselor walked with perfect posture. She pegged her for a dancer. Faith noticed things like that.

They came to a conference room with a big round table in the center. Miss Flemings invited them to sit in the comfy burgundy chairs that encircled the table.

Faith looked across the table and for the first time noticed the counselor's eyes. They were a copper-greenish color with a softness to them. Miss Flemings looked back at Faith, and at that moment Faith saw something else. The counselor knew. It was as if she knew something more than most people, and her eyes told Faith that she knew something about what Faith was going through.

Miss Flemings asked, "What brings you to Hollow Hills Middle School?"

Faith opened her mouth to reply, but her mother spoke first. "We've just moved from Greenvale after a family divorce, and Faith is very excited to begin at her new school."

Miss Flemings looked at Faith with that knowing look she probably gave to all newly divorced families and said, "Well, it's good to have you here, and if there's anything I can do to support you, let me know. First, I need to know how old you are, Faith."

She peered through her long, dark bangs and answered, "I just turned thirteen in July."

"Okay, so that puts you in eighth grade at our school. Am I right?"

"Yeah, you're right. Somehow I was able to finish seventh grade," Faith answered.

Mrs. Clancy added, "It was a bit difficult, what with the divorce, and then there were some problems at school."

Miss Flemings said, "That's definitely something we might want to talk about. Right now we can get started by completing the registration forms, and then you'll be given a tour from two of our student guides. Excuse me one moment." She stepped out of the room and disappeared around the corner.

Faith noticed her mother looking at her.

"What?" Faith asked, hoping she noticed the extra layer of black eyeliner and midnight-black mascara she had so carefully applied.

Faith heard footsteps approaching from the long hallway that led back to the main office. Two students appeared.

Miss Flemings returned with her forms and introduced the boy and girl. "Faith, meet Robert and Lana, two of our peer helpers who are here to give you a tour. Why don't you begin now while your mother completes the registration forms?"

Faith joined the two peer helpers. While they talked, Faith noticed many things about the school, like the mouth-watering aroma of chocolate coming from the home economics classroom. Just outside the door leading to technology shop she heard loud, shrill noises from drills and saws. She got a whiff of something familiar, reminding her of the Christmas tree lot outside Durham's Hardware. The tour rounded a corner, and Faith heard the sound of guitars strumming.

The helpers led Faith down a long hallway. The scent of french fries wafted past their noses and grew stronger as they neared the cafeteria. They entered and watched the cook dunking a metal strainer of fries into a vat of seriously hot oil. Out of the corner of her eye, Faith was distracted by someone coming through the door. She turned around to see. No one was there. *That's strange*, she thought.

The tour continued through the courtyard doors to the athletic fields behind the school. There was a soccer field, football field, and baseball field. They walked to the bleachers, stepped to the top, and sat down. The two helpers talked about the clubs and sports the school had to offer.

Robert asked, "Faith, are you interested in joining any clubs, such as the school newspaper club, cross-country running, chess club, home arts, or computer club?"

"Well, I'm not too sure," Faith answered, trying to be polite. "They sound okay, but I think I might start with getting used to my new home and living out in the country. I came from the city, where it wasn't quite this green. It was busy, lots of traffic, and the air was a bit pungent from car exhaust and pollution. The air is so fresh here, but right now I smell something burning. The scent is really nice, though."

Lana answered, "Someone must have their fireplace going. I believe they're burning cedar."

Robert, intent on sticking to his topic, said, "Faith, what about sports? We have volleyball, basketball, and track and field."

Faith replied, "Maybe later in the year." She was distracted by a figure to the far left of the football field standing next to a tree. She flicked her bangs to the side so she could see better, and using a black scrunchie she found in her purse, she pulled her long, dark hair through to make a ponytail.

"What's over by that big tree?" Faith asked.

"That's a maple tree and a creek runs past it. Let's go take a look. You know, because we live on the Pacific coast, you'll find we have a lot of salmon-spawning creeks and streams. This is one of them. In the fall, the salmon make their way up from the ocean, and we just might see some today," Robert said.

As they walked, Lana said, "Oh, I forgot to tell you about cheerleading tryouts. Interested?"

Faith immediately thought about cheerleading tryouts at her former school, where a group of girls had bullied her, causing her to drop out, and eventually, due to a lot of other things, she dyed her auburn hair dark black, began lining her eyes with the darkest eyeliner, wore black all the time, and skipped a lot of school. It was like she disappeared into the shadows so nobody would notice her. She felt it was safer that way, being invisible to even her parents, who were constantly arguing and bringing up the word *divorce*.

Faith remembered the day the counselor at her former school sat down with her and said, "I've watched you go through quite a dramatic change. You know, you've been one of the school's star pupils, and I have a gut feeling something's going on. Is there anything you'd like to share with me?" Faith eventually told her about the cheerleader tryouts and the bullies, and to this day she can hear the counselor's words: "Look, Faith, you have a lot going for you. You're very pretty, you keep yourself in good shape, you're coordinated, and you would probably have made the squad. Those bullies needed you to drop out so they'd have a better chance of winning. It wasn't right. I only wish I would've found out sooner."

Lana repeated, "Faith, Faith! I said are you interested in trying out for cheerleader?"

Yanked out of her deep thoughts, Faith looked up and answered, "Cheerleading tryouts? I don't think so."

They cut diagonally across the football field, walked a few yards, and came to a large maple tree towering over a bubbling creek. Huge rocks sat on either side. Faith looked around for the figure she'd seen. *Gone. That's twice,* she thought. *First in the cafeteria and now another mystery.* She looked down at the creek and watched a fallen leaf float on top of the crystal-clear water.

Robert looked at his watch and said, "We'd better head back. Almost lunchtime. Oh, I forgot one thing. See that line of trees over there? It marks the beginning of the forest, which is also the boundary of the school. No one's allowed in that forest. Serious trouble if you do go beyond the tree line."

Faith and her mother drove home after the big tour. It wasn't as if they had to drive; it was a small town, and they were only a few blocks away. They were quiet. Faith thought her mom was probably thinking about the divorce, while she was thinking about that too and about how life was in the city and the events that had happened at her old school. She wondered if they were going to happen here.

She watched as they passed, one by one, the now familiar houses. Without fences, the wide-spreading yards seemed to blend into one another. Most of the houses were built of wood and seemed to sit quietly in front of the forested mountains of this little town of Hollow Hills near the Pacific Ocean.

On the day they arrived to move in, the sky had been dark with clouds hovering over winding roads. Drizzling rain dotted their windshield. Fog drifted in and out, making it difficult for

Faith's mother to navigate the unfamiliar roads. They finally found their house at the very tip of the dead-end road. A dark forest bordered the far side and on the other stood a seemingly frightening two-story gray house, the kind used for haunted house movies. No one lived there, and to this day it stands empty.

Faith thought, *Sometimes at night, I see a dim orangey-yellow glow in many of the windows of the gray house, making it look like candles are burning throughout. Our house isn't as frightening. It has four stained-glass windows, and when the sun shines, the house lights up with different colors. That's about all I like about this new house and town.*

There's a little garden in the front that Mom likes. She says it makes our one-story white house look charming. Our yard is massive, not like the patches of lawn in the city. It'd be cool to have a dog if we stay here, because there's not much of anything to do and it's not like I have thousands of friends or even a single one.

I should ask Mom to get me a dog for my birthday—or just any day for that matter. With a dog, I'd be able to explore the woods that border our yard. The trails look like they wind up and around the mountains, and a big dog would be a good hiking buddy. I've got it figured out. It might be okay to live here if I have a dog, a large dog, maybe something like a yellow lab, something to hug and something that will love me no matter what.

Later that evening Faith sat on her bed holding a large green and yellow book she'd taken from her shelf. She opened it to reveal a cutout in the center of the pages. Inside, she'd hidden her journal and pen.

She began writing:

Today, was my first day at Hollow Hills Middle. Mom took me to register and they gave me a tour. It's okay, I guess.

I noticed something strange, something mysterious. Something is there. Something more than just the students and teachers. I'm talking about something that was there, and then it wasn't. It happened twice. Oh, and the front door. I got a real zap from it. Oh, yeah, there's definitely something there and I'm going to find out what that something is.

And cheerleading? Not a chance!

Dad, I miss you. I wish things were the way they used to be. You said I would like it here. I hope I can trust that to be true. Right now I'm not so sure. I wish you were here. You'd like our huge front yard. We could practice throwing spirals, like we used to. I love you, Dad.

CHAPTER 2

Hollow Hills Explorers, Investigators of the Unknown

FAITH KEPT TO HERSELF AS SHE EASED INTO THE ROUTINE OF her new middle school. She had a feeling the school was hiding some mysteries and hoped she'd get some answers soon. She'd seen the headlines in the morning newspaper that the real harvest moon was going to be the largest seen in a decade; not only that, it was a blue moon. This was a very rare event.

Faith soon discovered that most students weren't interested in harvest moons, blue moons, or any moons, for that matter. They preferred Friday night football games and who was going and rooting for their team. She felt like an outsider at the spirit assemblies that were held before the games. In the hallways and on the fields, clusters of kids huddled together, whispering amongst themselves, making it clear she wasn't welcome into their cliques. She didn't care, though, since she didn't want to be part of any lame group anyway.

Fortunately, she'd met Dalton and things began to look up for her. Dalton was a member of the Hollow Hills Explorers, HHE for short. This club investigated the unknown. To this day there were only three members, Dalton, Finn, and Oliver.

At lunchtime, Dalton and Faith were standing in line waiting as the cook sliced a pepperoni pizza.

"Why don't you join me and a couple of friends out at the creek?" Dalton asked Faith. "We usually eat our lunch there, and it's also our usual HHE meeting place."

Faith replied, "Sure, I guess." She was wearing jeans and a dark-blue shirt. She no longer spent the time to put on black eyeliner but wouldn't leave the house without mascara.

Dalton joined the other two HHEs. "Hey, guys! This is Faith. She's new."

Finn and Oliver gave her a nod hello while glancing at Dalton with a look of suspicion.

"She's cool," Dalton said. "She was in the lunch line and saw the book I was holding about the moon. She's already read it and started telling me stuff I didn't even know!"

Faith said hello and muttered, "I always liked astronomy. People think I'm weird." She shrugged.

"That's not weird," Finn said.

"Most girls don't care about how the early explorers traveled across the ocean without a GPS," she said. "And I don't care about celebrities and clothes."

"Faith, I think you look good," Dalton said. "Besides, the way I see things, it's more about who you are, not what you wear."

"Thanks, Dalton," Faith replied.

They spread out along the creek and sat on the rocks. Faith chose a large rock with a ledge that stuck out over the water. She put her lunch on the ledge and looked over. The water was so clear she could see fish making their way upstream as they fed on algae or the odd bug (and the not so odd bug). She watched the water meander around rocks as it made its way down the creek bed.

Finn asked, "Hey, Faith, what do you know about the full moon happening tonight? Did you know it's called a blue moon?"

Faith replied, "Yeah, I can't wait to see it! It's the largest full moon in a long time and a blue moon! Unbelievable! I wouldn't miss it for anything."

Finn said with anticipation, "Yeah, they say it's going to be awesome."

"I can't wait," Oliver added. "I'm going to bring my telescope."

Dalton said sadly, "Yeah, I have a football practice and might have to miss it."

Finn said, "Well don't go. You can miss one practice, can't you? I mean, it's not like they're going to miss you if you just happen to sneak out while they're running drills."

"Can't do it. What if the coach kicks me off the team?" Dalton asked.

"That'd only happen once in a 'blue moon,'" Finn joked, and everyone laughed.

"Ha-ha," Dalton chided.

Oliver said, "Well, we'll wait right here until you get out, and then we'll all go to the Hollows and watch the moon from there. We'll have a really good view."

Faith picked at her salad while noticing Dalton look at Oliver, who looked at Finn before all three looked in her direction.

It was Dalton who spoke, though. "Hey, Faith, would you like to join our club? It's exclusive."

Finn jumped in, "We do a lot of hiking and exploring into what we call the unknown, and we use my special GPS to search for treasures that have been hidden out in fields and forests."

Oliver added. "Last week we tramped through a pond we found up Snake Hill Trail and collected samples. We took them home and looked at them through my microscope. It was a real eye opener to discover what we can see with the microscope. All these little organisms floating around. We also search for agates and polish them up in Dalton's tumbler. We've got quite a collection."

Finn said, "We're meeting tonight to observe the moon."

Oliver said, "Finn and I will be here around six. Do you think you can make it?"

Faith was amazed. Already her second day of school and she'd made friends, and they even asked her to join their club and go on an adventure.

"I'll see what I can do. I don't know if my mom will go for it, being I'm new to the school and all and she doesn't know you."

"No problem," Oliver said. "We'll be at your house at six o'clock, and we'll meet your mother. She'll see we're decent enough and that we can be trusted."

"Okay," Faith replied, realizing three guys had just invited themselves to meet her mother. *I'm going to have to prepare her for this. What am I going to tell her?* she thought.

She asked the boys, "What will I say? Yeah, Mom, I made new friends and they're all guys and we're going to go out in the dark of night into the forest or some scary place like that and watch the moon. Right!"

Oliver chimed in, "Not to worry. We're pretty good with moms. You'll see." Oliver handed his iPad to Faith. "Here, type in your address."

Just then the bell rang. She typed in her address and said, "What's your plan?"

"No time. Just trust us," Oliver replied.

"Okay, see you at six."

Faith quickly gathered her things and walked across the field. Her walk soon turned into a run as she thought how exciting this was and wondered what it would mean to be part of this group.

CHAPTER 3

Night of the Blue Moon Rising

It was the night of the blue moon. Anticipation with a hint of suspense was in the air for all those awaiting the rising of the moon. For Faith, the idea of asking her mother if she could go to this place in the woods with some friends she just met today was an idea that just might not take off—not to mention the new friends were all guys.

She thought as she sat on her bed finishing her homework, *I might as well not even ask. Mom will probably never let me go out in a new neighborhood late at night. Wait—I'm defeating the idea and defeating myself before I even ask. I promised myself I would be more positive, more assertive, and no longer a victim. The least I can do is try.*

Faith was setting the table when her mom asked her, "How was school today?"

Faith replied, "It was good," and she paused to think how she would say what she wanted to say, but her mother had something to share.

"I have a surprise to share with you. I got a job today. So I guess it's been a good day all around."

"Oh, Mom, that's great! When do you start?"

"Monday. So I have quite a lot to read up on between now and next week."

Silence surrounded the dinner table as they ate their salads. Faith was thinking and thinking and thinking about what she would say. *Be positive. Think positive*, she told herself.

She finished her salad, and just before starting on her chicken, she thought, *Now or never—here goes!* "Mom, I met some new friends at school today."

"Oh, that's good, honey," her mother said while reading over some paperwork she had placed next to her plate.

Faith knew her mother wanted to impress her new boss, so it was going to be difficult to get her attention. "Yeah, they're going to come over and we're going to hang out," she casually slipped in.

"That's nice. What time?"

"Six o'clock okay?"

Without looking up she replied, "Oh, of course."

"I think these friends," Faith said, making sure she didn't say guys, not too sure how her mother would react to the fact they were all boys, "have the same interests as me. It's good being able to talk about things you like without being called 'weird.'"

"Yes, I think it's very important that you're able to make good friends. Maybe Hollow Hills Middle School will be just the place for you."

When the doorbell rang at precisely 6:00 p.m., Faith dashed down the stairs. Her mother was coming from the kitchen to answer it but stopped with a look of surprise.

"Don't you look nice," she said, pointing to Faith's pink T-shirt and freshly washed jeans.

"Thanks," Faith mumbled, heading to the door.

"And I like that you're not wearing so much mascara and eyeliner."

Faith smiled and opened the door. There stood Oliver and Finn. She invited them in and introduced them to her mother.

"Come on in, boys," her mother said, motioning them to the living room where she had placed a bowl of chips and a plate piled high with chocolate chip cookies on the coffee table.

Instead of diving in, Oliver and Finn sat on the couch.

"Help yourself," Faith's mother said.

Oliver looked at Faith. "We can't stay for too long," he said.

"Oh?"

Faith held her breath as Finn spoke up. "We're going to study the full moon." He motioned to his telescope.

"Mom," Faith interjected, "it's a blue moon tonight. That doesn't happen very often."

"So what are your plans for the evening?" Mrs. Clancy asked.

Finn spoke up. "I've brought my telescope and GPS, and Oliver's brought his new iPad. We're going to study the full moon. Are you aware that it's also a blue moon? That makes it a very rare event."

Oliver added, "That's right. It rarely happens as the full moon appears every 29.53 days, making it full approximately once a month. That means that each season has three full moons. That leaves eleven days leftover each year, which adds up to give an extra full moon every two or three years, so one of the seasons will have four full moons. For that season, the third one of those four is called the blue moon. To make it simple, some people say a blue moon is when there are two full moons in one month, which is correct but not quite accurate."

Mrs. Clancy asked, "But why do they call it 'blue'?"

Oliver quickly replied, "What makes the moon the color blue? Well, I've read that sometimes a blue moon can be caused by volcanic dust or fire particles. It's also been said that the word blue had its origins in the word *blewe*, spelled b-l-e-w-e, which means 'to betray.' So people seeing two moons in a particular month or four moons in that season felt the extra moon betrayed them."

Mrs. Clancy said, "It reminds me of a song I love." She started humming the melody to "Blue Moon."

Faith wished her mother would stop. She was embarrassing her. But then she noticed a look of sorrow on her Mom's face. As though reading Faith's mind, her mother looked over at her and quickly said, "Oh, goodness, I am sorry!"

That's when it occurred to Faith that maybe the divorce didn't just make her sad, it made her mother sad.

Faith laughed it off and said, "It's good to hear you singing again, Mom." She just wished it hadn't been in front of her new friends.

Mrs. Clancy smiled at the boys and said, "You know, boys, it's so very nice to meet you, and it's so nice of you to include Faith. You both look very responsible. Can you tell me about your GPS, Finn? It looks pretty sophisticated."

"Well," Finn started, "it's more specialized than the simple ones found in cars. GPS—which stands for 'global positioning satellite'—picks up signals from more than one satellite and leads me to a very, very specific location based on its coordinates in degrees and minutes of latitude and longitude. It's very precise."

"How did you get started using a highly specialized device like that?" she asked.

"Oh, well, you see, my father likes to hike and explore, so he wanted to make sure my brother and I could handle ourselves and survive in the forested mountains to the north of here. So one day he took us to the mountains and we hiked for a bit, and then he said he was going to see if we could find our way back. My brother was able to find his way back just like that, but I just kind of froze. I have no internal directional abilities. After a while my father and brother both came back into the forest, only to find me in the exact same spot they'd left me in."

"You mean to say you were alone in the mountains and expected to find your way out? Were you frightened?" Mrs. Clancy asked.

"Oh yeah, I was more than frightened. I was terrified. There are bears and cougars up there. So Oliver here helped me, and we researched GPS devices and found this super one. So now I can go anywhere knowing exactly where I am, and I can find my way out of any difficult spot. I always have it with me. I'm never lost. For my birthday, my Dad has promised me a 'wearable'. It's a watch with a GPS display. Oh, and I now participate in geo-caching and I've found treasures all over. But that's another story."

Mrs. Clancy replied, "Well, you'll have to tell me more about your treasure hunts another time, but it sounds like you turned a difficulty into a real plus. Now why don't you two boys have some chips and cookies? I need to return to my den and do some reading. It was nice to meet you."

Faith quickly asked, "Mom, would it be okay if I join Oliver and Finn?"

Finn added, "We're going to a place called the Hollows. It's behind the school. No worries about us getting lost because I have my GPS."

Mrs. Clancy smiled at Finn and replied, "Yes, I think it's okay. Be back no later than ten thirty. Okay?"

"Okay, Mom, thanks," Faith said as she rushed to get a bag to pack up the cookies and chips.

Once outside and on their way, Finn asked, "So we did all right?"

Faith replied, "Couldn't have gone any better. All the tech equipment added a nice touch. My mom was really impressed. Now where's this place you guys call the Hollows?"

Finn said, "Come on, we'll show you!"

They reached the school and spotted Dalton near the front doors.

"Hey, Dalton," Finn yelled. "Are you coming with us?"

"Hey, guys—and Faith, good to see you. Yeah, I finished practice, went home, grabbed something to eat, and headed

out with Keeper," he said, pointing to his dog, a border collie. "Faith, I'd like you to meet Keeper. Keeper, shake a paw!"
Keeper sat and raised his right paw. "Go ahead, Faith. He wants
you to shake his paw."

"Hi, Keeper." Faith took hold of his paw and gave it a shake.
"I like his name. How'd you come up with it?"

"Our family fosters dogs from the local shelter, and Keeper,
only a puppy then, was one of our fosters," Dalton explained.
"As we waited for someone to come along and adopt, the little
guy found a way into our hearts and we decided to keep him.
So we named him Keeper."

"That's a good name for him," Faith said, admiring his soft
black and white coat as she rubbed him behind his ears. Keeper
stood and wagged his tail.

"So are you ready to go to the Hollows to see the full blue
moon?" Dalton asked.

"Ready," she said.

"Okay, let's go," Dalton directed.

They walked behind the school, cut to the left, and came
to the football field. A rosy haze of misty fog hung low across
the field like a soft, downy blanket. They crossed as if they were
walking on a cloud. The mist swirled around their legs like
will-o'-the-wisps.

A tree line ran along the far side of the football field, marking
the beginning of the forest. Huge cedars, alders, and a few deciduous trees stood reaching to the sky. Dalton walked along, searching
for an opening. With a quick left turn he entered the forest.

Faith stopped and said, "Hey, wait you guys. I don't know
if this is such a good idea. We're not supposed to go in here!"

"What are you talking about?" Finn asked.

"On my first day, when I registered, the student tour guides pointed it out to me."

"Look, Faith, that rule's just for school hours. We've been here before and nothing's ever happened," Oliver reassured her.

Faith looked at Oliver, who wore a very serious expression. She wanted to believe he was being truthful. "Okay. Go ahead, I'll follow you,."

The opening led to a trail lined with tall trees on either side; their branches stretched out, forming a canopy overhead. Soft bark mulch and pine needles covered the trail. Faith could feel the softness as the path gave beneath her sneakers. A blanket of emerald green covered the surrounding ground. Darkened moss crept up and over fallen logs. Yellowish wild mushrooms dotted the forest floor. Ferns reached up among logs, and witch's beard hung down from the underside of branches.

A silence enveloped the group of four explorers. When they stepped on a twig, a simple snap was magnified and made a loud crunch. An eagle whistled from somewhere far away. A crow cawed across the forest. Another echoed his call.

The air heavy with humidity dampened Faith's skin. She made note of the fresh scent of the forest and took a deep breath, filling her lungs with the fresh, humid forest air. It wasn't like the smell of car exhaust she was assaulted with when she waited at intersections in the city.

She quietly said to the others, "This is so different from where I used to live. I'm definitely going to like it here. Are we getting close to this hollow place?"

"Not much farther," Finn answered. "Only about ninety steps north according to the readings on my GPS."

Faith trailed behind Oliver on a path that curved around huge gray boulders and fallen trees with trunks the size Faith had never seen before. She came upon logs that stretched far across the forest floor, creating giant zigzag patterns. Faith looked up to see strange beings, only to realize they were really tree branches appearing ready to reach out and grab them. She veered around tree stumps with notches that looked like eyes watching them.

Carrrrrrunch! A branch crackled somewhere close by. All chirps and caws ceased. Suddenly everything was hushed. The group froze, looking at one another. Keeper, the border collie, raised his head, his tail in the air, still and taut, signaling the group of potential danger. After a minute of total silence, Dalton gave the signal to continue and the group forged on.

A few more steps and Dalton, in the lead, called out, "We're here."

"Finally," Oliver replied.

Faith came to the end of the path and saw that it opened up into a clearing.

"This is why it's called 'the Hollows,'" Finn announced, sweeping his hand from left to right.

Faith turned around in a circle and saw hollowed-out trees, some standing three feet tall, others between ten and twenty feet, completely surrounded the group.

"Look!" Faith called. "They have eyes and mouths. It's a bit ghoulish."

Oliver explained, "These trees were logged more than a century ago. Where you see eyes and mouths, they're actually notches axed out by loggers. They'd insert planks called springboards that they could stand on while cutting the trees. Over the years the notches show signs of weathering. They grow moss and take on a bit of character. Watch this." He looked to the ground and chose two round, nearly white rocks. Then he selected just the right tree and stuck the rocks into the notches. The tree stared back at him, its new white "eyeballs" resting in its dark sockets.

"Actually," Oliver continued, "we're standing in what was once the loggers' camp. If we were to dig, we might find an old tin cup or fork. Now get this. I was researching the area and found a picture of the loggers and a story about this camp. It mentioned how one of the loggers had disappeared during a lightning storm—never to be seen again."

Finn joined in, "What do you mean disappeared? You don't just disappear. Did they even look for him, or did they just say, 'Oh, well he's gone, get back to work'?"

Oliver answered, "It said they searched the entire area for three days and had absolutely no leads. It was like something grabbed the guy and disappeared with him."

Finn added, "Maybe a cougar. They say cougars have an enormously large territory they call their own."

Oliver went on. "It was reported that often when they slept in their tents they'd hear something walking around their camp. Scrunch-scrunch-scrunch."

Goosebumps crawled up and down Faith's arms. The hair on her neck tingled.

A twig snapped in the forest. Another one. Keeper froze. The little hairs on his stiffened ears twitched. He sniffed and growled a low "grrrrrrrr."

"Maybe it's a cougar," Faith said.

Finn said, "Maybe it's the ghost of the logger."

Oliver continued, "He was actually quite young, in his teens. They said maybe fifteen years old. His mother had just died, and the father didn't want to leave him behind with his aunt, so he brought him to the camp to learn the trade. It was late in the afternoon when he disappeared. He was last seen working with his axe on a small tree south of camp just before a storm rumbled in and hit the camp with lightning and thunder."

Another snap.

Everyone jumped. They turned in the direction of the noise.

Keeper growled again and let out a small bark "Grrrrrrr-ruf." He poked his nose in the air, checking for scents.

Faith said, "That's him."

"Come on, you guys," Oliver said in an attempt to squelch the ghostly anxiety. "That's probably just a raccoon heading out for his nightly rendezvous. Now we came here to observe the blue moon, so let's get things set up." He reached into his bag, pulled out flashlights, and handed them out. The Hollows lit up. Light beams flashed back and forth. The Hollow Hills Explorers began setting up their blue-moon camp.

Faith heard branches snapping. She looked up and saw stars popping out and knew the moon was nearly ready to make its appearance. The night couldn't be better for watching the skies. The explorers had arrived just in time because darkness was setting in fast.

Dalton unrolled tarps and blankets, spread them out in the center of their makeshift camp, and everyone found a place.

Oliver took out his notebook and logged onto his favorite astrophysicist site. He wanted to know the exact position of the stars and the precise point on the horizon where the moon would soon make its appearance.

Finn assembled his telescope just outside the corner of the blankets and then checked his position on his GPS. He sat next to Oliver so he could get the precise readings when Oliver reported.

Faith and Dalton found a place and sat down, legs crossed, watching and waiting. Keeper curled up between the two.

The HHE club was ready for the full blue moon.

Dalton quietly asked, "So how do you like your new school, Faith?"

"It's good. I'm glad I transferred. I was a bit concerned at first, but the people seem pretty nice."

"Well, some are, but we do have the odd bullies, and there are cliques, but we try to avoid them," Dalton joked.

"Have you ever been bullied?" Faith asked him.

"No, but they pick on our friend Finn here once in a while," he replied. "His glasses. They're pretty thick. He's very smart, though. Reads a lot. There's probably nothing he doesn't know."

Finn said, "Yeah, bullies can be really cruel."

"Have you ever reported to the teachers or principal?" Faith asked.

Dalton answered, "Of course. You know what they tell him? They tell him to ignore the bullies, making it less fun for them. That's supposed to make them stop."

Faith said, "And do they?"

"No way," Finn replied.

"Well, what goes around comes around. I've read somewhere that what you put out comes back to you."

"What do you mean?" Dalton asked,

Faith answered, "Well, if you do something mean to someone, something bad will happen to you The same goes for if you do something nice—something nice will happen to you."

Oliver logged on to his computer and said, "Yes, that's a theory in physics. Sounds like Newton's third law of motion. You know, for every action, there's an equal and opposite reaction."

Sssssnaaap! The four of them jumped up, ready to run. Keeper was at full alert. His hackles stood on end. They looked toward the sound. It was getting closer.

Ssnaap! Another snap just outside the Hollows. A low growl could be heard coming from Keeper.

They waited. Nothing more.

Finn took a deep breath and whispered, "What do you think it was?"

I have no idea, "Dalton said, "but I see something even more interesting!" He ran over to the bag of chips, helping himself to a handful. "Oooh, chips!" he said. "I worked up an appetite. And what do we have here? Chocolate chip cookies? Yummm!"

"Homemade chocolate cookies," Faith said. "My mom made them."

"Nothing like homemade chocolate chip cookies," Dalton said.

"Mind if I have some chips?" Dalton asked politely.

"Help yourself," Faith answered

Snap! Another branch cracked.

They all turned. All was silent except Dalton crunching potato chips. Crunch, crunch, crunch.

Finn whispered, "Dalton, shhh. The chips, quiet."

Dalton froze with a full mouth and then garbled through the chips, "Are you expecting someone else?"

Oliver replied, "No, that's just it—we're not."

Dalton swallowed and then asked, "Well, who could it be? Nobody followed us. We made sure of that."

Finn whispered, "It's the ghost logger who haunts the Hollows."

"Boo!" Dalton shouted.

They all jumped. Oliver's chips flew high into the air and when they came down, Keeper was right there, snapping them up like a piranha.

"Hey! My chips," Oliver said as he watched Keeper search the ground for stray crumbs.

Dalton said, "I'm not so sure I believe in that ghostly logger thing."

"Well, whether you believe in it or don't believe in it doesn't mean it exists or doesn't exist," Oliver replied.

"Guys, it's no longer up for discussion. Look—there it is," Faith said quietly.

Everyone looked at her and followed her gaze straight to the forest.

"I don't see anything," Dalton said.

"Me neither. What'd you see?" Oliver asked.

"I saw something just behind the tree line. It was tall, just about your height, Dalton, and it looked like that misty fog we walked through on the football field. First I saw it move from that tree to behind that tall hemlock," she said pointing to the trees, "and then it crossed behind that short mossy stump to the trail. It seemed to disappear down the trail. Is there another way out of here? Because I don't want to go back down that trail."

"Oh, it was probably just someone's flashlight shining on the trees," Oliver said. "Watch. Faith, shine your flashlight on a tree near where you first saw him."

So Faith, trying to believe him, shined her light on the tree.

Oliver continued, "Okay, now slowly move it from that point across to the path."

She did.

Oliver asked, "So what do you think? Look pretty similar to what you saw? Now remember, each of the flashlights are different and may give a bigger light, a stronger light, a softer light, or whatever."

Finn said, "Let me shine my light there." He made a similar pattern.

Everyone had a turn, and then Oliver asked, "Could that be what you saw?"

Faith hesitantly tried her best to see what they were saying. "Well, I'm not so sure. It wasn't exactly what I saw, but maybe two flashlights had crossed, or a bit of the forest mist or will-o'-the-wisps had been there at the same time. It's possible. But still, I'm not so sure."

Just then Finn yelled out, "There it is!"

Everyone was startled and turned in his direction.

"The moon! The blue moon!" he exclaimed.

Everyone turned to face the eastern horizon and watch as the moon peaked over the horizon line, growing bigger and bigger, rising higher and higher until it seemed to fill half the horizon. It was so bright and strong that it shined right through the densely forested area, illuminating stumps and casting horrifying shadows. Soon it rose above the Hollows and seemed to rest on top of taller stumps like a big, fat, old orange cat sitting on a worn picket fence.

"Wow!" Dalton exclaimed, "I've never seen the moon that gigantic before."

"That's massive!" Oliver yelled.

"This is great! Hey, let's view it through the telescope!" Finn shouted. He put his eye to the viewer, adjusted its height and magnification, turned a few knobs, and said loudly, "Unbelievable! You can see everything!"

"Can I take a look?" Oliver asked.

"Absolutely!"

"Unreal! It's like we're just a few miles away. I can see the Kepler Crater. It's supposed to be twenty miles in diameter!" Oliver exclaimed. "Here, Faith—you've got to see this."

Faith took a look and didn't say a thing for a long time. Then she said in a quiet voice, "Never, ever in my life did I ever think I'd be seeing the moon this close." She moved away from the telescope and continued, "I mean, I've read about the moon in books and researched it on the net, but this, this is real! It's not on a computer screen, not on paper. This is live. It's awesome!"

So everyone took a turn looking at the moon. They used the Internet to access live feed from NASA.

Dalton said, "Hey, guys, we're right here. We don't need the net. This is live!"

Yes, they were right there looking at the real thing. They stood there with mouths open, minds taking it all in as they watched in awe, witnessing something rare and so absolutely spectacular. Time seemed to stand still.

However, as they observed this spectacle, Faith felt as though they were being watched!

The moon rose to new heights, filling the sky with bright amber light. In contrast, the darkness looked darker, stars shined brighter, and Venus made a brilliant accent to the moon. The sky twinkled like luminous jewels.

Faith could see what she thought was a satellite moving in slow motion across the sky. Realizing it was late, she came out of her moon trance. "What time is it? Does anyone know?"

Finn, checking his cell phone, replied, "It's ten fifteen."

Faith exclaimed, "I have to go! I have to be home by ten thirty!" And as she turned, she saw movement behind the trees. She didn't say a thing. Instead, she turned to see the boys taking down the camp with great speed, as though they'd done it many times before. After all, they were the Hollow Hills Explorers.

Oliver dismantled the telescope like a practiced army lieutenant dismantles a gun, and Finn marked their position with longitude and latitude on his new global positioning satellite. Blankets were rolled up and chips and cookie bags stashed in their garbage bag.

"We always practice CITO," Finn explained to Faith.

"What's that?"

In unison, the boys said, "'Cache in, trash out!'" They all laughed.

In no time at all the group had broken down the camp and were headed toward the tree line. Faith wondered if the boys were thinking about the apparition like she was. She couldn't get it out of her mind.

CHAPTER 4
Apparitions Appear

EARLY MORNING SUNSHINE STREAKED THROUGH THE STAINED-glass window, casting colors onto the white squares of the kitchen floor. Faith and her mother cooked up a big Saturday morning breakfast. They carried plates of cheesy omelets and toasted English muffins to the table and placed them next to a bowl of plump blueberries.

"How'd last night go? Were you able to see the blue moon?" Mrs. Clancy asked.

"Yeah, we had a good time. The moon was amazing," Faith replied.

"I appreciate your being in by ten thirty. I don't want to have to worry about you."

"You know, it might help if I had my own cell phone," Faith hinted as she popped a ripe, juicy blueberry into her mouth. "I could just look at it every now and then. We were just so into watching the moon that time seemed to disappear," she said and thought, *Something else disappeared too.*

Faith continued popping blueberries, getting farther and farther away from her mouth. *I'm definitely not going to tell Mom about the figure behind the trees. That conversation would probably go something like this: Oh, yeah, Mom, there was this apparition that walked behind the trees. It hung out there until we had to leave and then … well, I just don't know where it went. You know what else? I'm the only one who saw it. They all thought it was just a reflection from flashlights shining on the mist, but I know it wasn't.*

Faith watched butter melting into the holes on her muffin and thought, *No way will I tell Mom about this. She probably wouldn't let me see my new friends again, and she'd probably take me to see that doctor again. It's not the first time I've been able to see things others can't.*

Ms. Clancy spread butter on her muffin until it was smooth as icing. She broke the silence. "Okay. Well, makes sense, seeing how you got in on time. I know you're trying to be responsible now, and I think you're ready for your own phone. Actually, it might be a good idea. I'd like to be able to contact you in case I have to work late, and I'd like to know if you're staying after school for activities." She cut into her steaming omelet, cheese oozing out and slowly spreading on her plate. "We'll go out a little later and look for one. Then we'll go to the store and pick up some groceries. Now tell me more about that blue moon."

Faith was cutting off a piece of her omelet, drawing it up to her mouth and watching as a warm piece of cheese stretched from her plate up into the air. She rolled it around her fork, slid it into her mouth, chewed it slowly, savoring the flavors, and then answered, "Oh, Mom, it was unbelievable. It was unlike anything I've ever seen before. It's so hard to describe. It was huge, and through Finn's telescope we could see the lunar landscape. Oliver had his laptop, and we navigated through NASA's website and were able to identify craters. I learned so much. The best part was the brightness and the deepest orange color I'd ever seen. It definitely wasn't blue."

Her mother laughed and then asked, "Where did you go to view the moon? Oh, I forgot the juice. Go ahead, I'm listening," she said as she walked over, picked up the two glasses of grape juice still sitting on the counter, and carried them back to the table.

"We went behind the school across the football field. There's a path that leads through the forest and comes to a clearing that's surrounded by old hollow tree stumps. They call it the Hollows. That's where we set up. Oh, and thanks for the chips and cookies. The guys loved 'em."

"Well, thank you. Glad you enjoyed them," she said, taking a sip of her juice. "This forest—is it a safe place? Is there any wildlife to be concerned with?"

Faith had started drinking her grape juice and nearly choked when her mother said the word "wildlife" because she immediately thought about the flashlight apparition, but instead she said, "Oh, it's okay. Maybe a raccoon or squirrel, but nothing really to speak of."

"I'm talking about your friends. Did any of them get wild and do anything I might be concerned with?" Mrs. Clancy asked.

"Not even, Mom. They're not like that. Not like my old school. I know there was a lot of that going on, but these guys are all right."

"So it was just you and the two boys? They seem bright. Probably a common link for all of you."

"Oh, yeah. These guys are smart. Oh, one more friend showed up. His name's Dalton. He plays on the football team and has the cutest dog, Keeper. You know, I'd really love to have a dog ..."

"Hold on a second there—another boy? Are there any girls in this group?" she asked.

"I don't know. I didn't ask. Maybe I haven't met them yet." She thought of the apparition. *Maybe it's a "she." This is something I'm going to have to research.*

Faith spent the afternoon with her mom, first looking for a new cell phone and then grocery shopping. Faith knew money was a bit tight, so she didn't go for the high-priced phone. Actually, she felt lucky just getting one and liked the fact her mom told her she was acting responsibly now. Big change from her last school where she'd become rebellious, even stopped doing her homework. That was when her parents were fighting every night. Faith started hanging out with the wrong crowd and coming home late and getting into serious trouble. Things were different now, and she felt good about herself.

The two shoppers found a grocery store nearby. It was smaller than the one in the city, and everything was in a different place than they were used to, so they had to do quite a bit of searching. They found the fruits and vegetables were fresher and there was a large selection of organic foods.

Although Faith enjoyed spending time with her mom, she kept thinking about last night. She really wanted to get home as soon as she possible so she could do some research on apparitions.

It was late in the afternoon when they'd finished shopping, and Faith had to do some chores before supper. When she finished her chores, she went into the kitchen to help with dinner.

Thick, juicy hamburgers sizzled in the frying pan. A pot of beans bubbled nearby.

"Faith can you please help me set the table?" she asked, motioning to the plates, glasses of milk, and condiments.

Faith began setting the table for one of her favorites meals. "Wait, something's missing. Where are the chips?"

"Right there." Her mother pointed to a plate of darkened, crinkled chips. "Try them."

Faith cautiously tasted a corner of one. "They're all right. They're different, but not bad. What are they?"

"They're kale chips. They're supposed to be very healthy. I kind of like them."

Faith had her eyes on the hamburgers. Her mom made them extra thick. When they sat down to eat, she topped her hamburger with lettuce, sliced tomatoes, and lots of ketchup.

After dinner, Faith went quickly to her bedroom and began doing research. She didn't find anything really substantial, only that apparitions might be ghostly visions.

Before going to sleep, she took out her journal and pen and wrote.

Last night, I went with the Hollow Hills Explorers to this place called 'the Hollows' to see the blue moon. It's supposed to be a really rare event. But a strange thing happened I saw something eerie and think it might be an apparition, which means something like a ghost or spirit. The weird thing is only I could see this apparition. I wonder why I was the only one who could see this ghostly thing? Will I ever see this thing again? I think tomorrow I'll go out to the Hollows and investigate.

CHAPTER 5

Ghost Seekers Meet the Dust-Spewing Bullies

It was a brisk Sunday morning. Faith, the new member of the Explorers Club, was preparing to spend the afternoon checking out the Hollows. She filled her backpack with cookies, her new phone, and a notebook and pen as she prepared to go out to explore the Hollows by herself.

"Mom, I'm going out exploring."

"Where do you intend to do this exploring?"

"I thought I'd go out to the school and take the trail to the Hollows."

"Is it safe to go by yourself?"

"Yes, I'll be safe. I'll take my new phone with me."

"Well, call me if you need me, okay?"

"Okay, Mom. Thanks. I'll be back before dinner."

"How about you'll be back by four?"

"Sounds good. See ya." She grabbed her backpack, threw it over her shoulders, and was off.

Heading down the street, Faith noticed the mountains behind the school. Orange and yellow leaves dotted the forest. Fall was here, and a slight chill reminded her that she'd better start bringing a sweatshirt.

As she approached Maple Park, she spotted Finn and Oliver sitting on crudely built swings that hung from the branches of an old oak. They were looking down at the ground, lazily dragging their feet in dirt and dead leaves. They spun in circles, slowly going in one direction and then the other. Just a lazy September day of spinning and dragging in dusty dirt.

Faith crossed the grassy area and said, "Hey, guys, what brings you out to the park?"

Startled, Finn looked up. "Hey, Faith, how's it goin'? We're just hangin' out."

Oliver joined in. "Hi, Faith. We were just talking about Friday night and how incredible it was."

Faith replied, "It truly was. A night I definitely won't forget."

Finn stammered, "Well, yeah, and … uh … well, we wanted you to know that we found something out and … uh …"

Oliver interrupted with, "Yeah, what he's trying to say is that we believe you. We believe you … might have seen something, and that something might be significant."

Finn interrupted. "Yeah, that something may also have been seen by someone else."

"What? What are you talking about? And who are you talking about?"

Oliver said, "Well, we spent yesterday afternoon at the library going through the archives of old local newspapers, and we found information on a fellow who'd been a logger. He'd settled in this area and claimed he saw the young fellow who'd disappeared. The old logger thinks it was his ghost, and guess where he saw it?"

"Where?" Faith asked. "Where'd he see it?"

Oliver and Finn exclaimed at the same time, "Out by the Hollows."

"Out by the Hollows?" Faith repeated. "Right where we were on the night of the blue moon?"

Finn said, "Yes, yes, yes. You got it!"

Oliver went on. "So you're not the only one who's seen it or him or whatever it is."

Faith said, "Well, that makes me feel a lot better, like I'm not going crazy and seeing things that aren't there. But you guys didn't see it?"

Finn shook his head. "Nope."

Oliver said, "No, but there's always a next time—maybe not a blue moon but a full moon."

Faith shrugged. "Hey, do you think it only appears on the night of full moons, or just blue moons?"

Oliver thought for a moment. "Well, I guess we'll find out in approximately 29.53 days. Just keep your eyes open."

Faith added, "Yesterday I did a lot of research on apparitions, and some sites say it could be a form of a human mind or spirit. So if we're correct, then it's the young guy's mind making itself visible in the form of that white will-o'-the-wispy shape."

Oliver suggested, "How 'bout we go back there right now and you tell us exactly what you saw and where you saw it. This way I can take notes and document everything."

Faith replied, "That's exactly where I was heading. Ready when you are!"

Finn said, "Well, what are we waiting for? Let's go."

So the three went off on one of their scientific adventures. They wanted to prove whether this apparition did or didn't exist and the possibility of it being the actual spirit of the young fellow.

They arrived at the school and made their way to the sports field behind the building. A group of boys down at the far end were playing a game of football.

Faith looked toward the group. "Hey, maybe Dalton's with those guys."

"No, I don't think so," Oliver said. "We called him this morning to see if he wanted to hang out with us, and his mother said he was busy with homework."

The explorers went the opposite way, crossed the field, and found the opening to the trail.

They hiked through the forest until they found the clearing encircled by the giant, hollowed-out stumps. In the afternoon fall sunlight, the stumps, with their long shadows, took on a different appearance. Faith was able to see exactly where the loggers had made their notches in the trees to insert their springboards.

She said, "Gee, these stumps don't look as scary as they did the other night. I could have sworn they had eyes and mouths. Now I can see the axed-out notches."

Finn replied, "Yeah, during the day everything seems more realistic, and at night everything looks creepier. We end up scaring ourselves."

Oliver, already taking notes, said to Faith, "So show us exactly where you saw the apparition."

"It was right over there." She walked to the trees. "I first saw him right here."

Oliver asked, "What'd he look like? Describe him to us."

"Hey, did you notice we're already calling it a him, a male?" Finn pointed out.

Oliver said, "You never know, and we haven't really proved anything yet."

Finn said, "How can we prove it, really? I think we're talking about ghosts and spirits. How do you prove that?"

Faith said, "You're right. It's almost like you have to just believe the person who saw it. You have to totally trust the person's word. So you actually have to trust me, my word. I wish you guys could have seen what I saw."

Oliver said, "Well, maybe if we focus and stay positive, we will."

Finn said a little impatiently, "Come on, Faith. Tell us what he looked like."

Faith said, "Okay, you want to know what he looked like? A description? There's not much." She walked to a hemlock tree that stood about twenty feet tall, its trunk nearly bare. She picked up a sharp rock, scraped it across the trunk, and then continued. "Okay, so first, when I saw him, he stood this high against this tree."

Finn said, "So just around five and a half feet. What else? Were his feet on the ground?"

Oliver said, "Give her time."

"The color was white, but it was a see-through white. And yes, his feet appeared to be near or on the ground."

Oliver said, "Sounds like a ghost to me. I wonder if ghosts ever come through in color."

Carrrrrunch. Snap. The sound of breaking branches came from deep within the forest.

Faith whispered, "Did you hear that?"

Oliver said, "Shhh."

Crrrunch. Snap, crrrrunch. It was getting closer.

Finn whispered, "It's coming from the trail."

Faith, Finn, and Oliver, not saying a word, using only their ears and their eyes, stood frozen just outside the tree line. They were exposed, in sight of anyone or anything that might make an appearance.

More crunching and crackling.

Their eyes were glued to the trail. Their ears, like submarine sonar instruments, listened for any slight sound. A muffled voice came from the forest. More than one. They were getting louder and louder.

The crackling and crunching became thunderous. The three explorers began backing away from the trail opening.

All of a sudden, four of the guys who'd been playing football exploded into the open space near the head of the trail.

Faith gasped, stumbled backward, and fell into a cluster of large green ferns.

Oliver jumped over a log and reached down to help her up.

Finn turned his head and murmured to Faith, "Oh no, it's Dustin, Jarrod, Randy, and Jeff. They're the last ones I'd ever want to run into out here in the forest."

"And what do we have here?" Jarrod boomed. The tall, sturdy athlete wore a black and fluorescent green shirt and towered a full head above his buddies.

"Yeah, what're you doin' here? Huh?" Randy, a short, muscular boy wearing a blue athletic sweatshirt, asked as he eyeballed the three.

Another stocky, beefed-up tough guy, Dustin, in an oversized orange and black striped rugby shirt walked closer and said, "Where's your other friend, the one with pop bottles for eyes?"

Dustin obviously didn't recognize Finn without his glasses.

The tough guys edged closer and closer. Then Dustin, leading the pack, caught his foot under a big branch lodged into the ground. Thud! The big guy hit the dirt. He didn't move. Everyone leaned forward to get a better look. Nothing. No movement.

Then, like a monster rising from the swamp and growing appendages from his armpits, Dustin's arms began moving like a bat's wings, stirring up dust. His immense hands reached out, palms flat on the ground, and then as though he was doing a push-up in gym class, he elevated his upper body and emitted a deep, loud growl: "Garrrrrumph." A huge dust ball spewed from his mouth, followed by a fit of coughing.

The others watched the coughing brown silhouette of what was once a black-and-orange-stripe-shirted athlete stand fully erect. As the dust settled around his black and silver running shoes, the big guy spat out a final ball of brown muddy slime and a garbled, "What the—"

The mob of tough guys burst out laughing—all except for one, of course. Their laughter sounded like a roaring belly laugh coming from one of the stump monsters deep in the forest. Jeff, Randy, and Jarrod laughed and laughed until they were rolling on the ground in their own cloud of dusty dirt.

Oliver, Finn, and Faith tried holding in their laughter, but it was impossible.

Dustin, the clumsy, slime-spitting tough guy said, "Hey, you idiots, cut it out."

This only made them laugh all the more.

"I'm outta here!" he yelled, obviously and utterly embarrassed this had happened in front of the new girl.

The other rolling toughies pushed themselves up and followed him.

The three ghost seekers, now stifling their laughter, watched as Dustin, Jarrod, Randy, and Jeff made their way down the trail in a big, brown cloud. When the team was far enough away, the three burst out with raucous laughter.

Amidst the laughter, Oliver said, "He fell really hard. But, you know—funny thing—I don't remember that stick being there." He pointed to the thick, sturdy branch sticking out at a diagonal to the ground.

Finn stopped his laughter. "Hey, you're right. I don't either. I forgot my glasses, and I'm sure I would have tripped over it. I'm always tripping over things, and that stick's right in the way."

All laughter stopped. Silence fell upon the Hollows like fog over a pumpkin field on a chilly October evening.

A lone tree frog croaked somewhere deep in the forest.

Oliver whispered, "So what are you thinking, Finn?"

"I don't know. I'm thinking, I'm thinking."

Faith walked to the suspect branch and gave it a tug. It came out so effortlessly that once again she stumbled backward, losing her balance and landing on the same bunch of ferns. "How could he have tripped on this? It was barely stuck in the ground."

Oliver helped her up and took the stick. He turned it over and over, inspecting it for signs of something. Evidence of the unknown.

Oliver went into investigator mode. "Seems like a regular old branch, but if it had been there when we came down the trail and out to the Hollows the other night, one of us probably would have tripped on it. That football player tripped on it right there in the opening of the trail. No," Oliver said, shaking his head. "No way. It definitely wasn't there. And it wasn't there when we arrived today."

Finn surmised, "Well, maybe someone was here this morning or yesterday, possibly throwing it for their dog. Dalton could have been out here with Keeper."

Finn inspected the stick, rolling it over and over. "Nope, no bite marks."

It was at this point that Faith finally decided to confide in the guys. "You know the other night when I told you I saw something, and everyone tried to be rational, coming up with reasons of something else I might have seen? Like flashlights crossing in the night? Well, that wasn't the only time I saw it."

Finn asked, "What are you saying? You saw it more than once?"

"Yes, when we were hurrying to leave. I saw it in the forest. It walked on top of one of the fallen trees and then down the trail until it disappeared."

Finn said, "Right. That ghost or whatever actually went down the trail seconds before us and I didn't see it?"

"That's right."

Oliver, furiously taking notes, said, "So you've seen him more than once—that might mean you just might see him again. Well, let's all keep our eyes open. You know what? I just thought of something. What if there's more than one way this apparition or ghost makes its presence known? Like not just visually."

Finn added, "What, like sounds? Or even placing something, like that stick, where someone like a bully just might trip over it?"

And with that revelation, the three of them looked at each other with mouths open in small oval shapes like the second half of a coyote's howl—ooooooh!

CHAPTER 6
Trusting the Explorers

FAITH LEANED AGAINST THE OLD MAPLE TREE IN FRONT OF THE school, watching students walk through the green framed school doors of Hollow Hills Middle School. Nothing. They merely walked through, just chatting away, on their way to lockers, meetings, or early morning practices. Nothing out of the ordinary happened. No lightning, no thunder, no reaction. *Okay,* she thought, *it's Monday, week two at my new school, and here I go through the green zapper.*

She looked around to see if anyone was coming. *Good, a break in traffic.* She casually walked toward the green front door and kept going, left foot through, right foot through—zzzz-zap! A rapid, mild jolt of electricity, like a snap from a rubber band, zapped her. Then she heard a rumble of thunder, the kind that happens during a summer rainstorm and you're count-ing the seconds after lightning strikes. Only this happened in a millisecond. She quickly turned around, walked back out, turned around again, and then walked back in. Zzzzap!

Interesting ... only when I enter, not when I exit, she thought as she walked down the hall to her locker. She hung her backpack inside and took out what she needed for classes.

"Hey, how's it goin'?" a voice from behind asked.

Faith turned around to find Dalton leaning against the lockers.

"You all right? You look like you just saw a ghost," he said, chuckling.

"Yeah, I'm all right. Look, I really don't want to talk about it."

"Okay, okay. Sorry. I guess I said the wrong thing."

"Look, it's not you. Really. I'll tell you later. Tell everyone to meet me at lunch."

"The creek?"

"The creek." With that she forced a smile. Dalton returned the smile, and she felt a flush from head to toe.

At lunch, the explorers gathered by the creek. A soft breeze carried leaves on its way, leaving some to rest on top of the water. A feeling of seriousness prevailed as everyone savored each bite of their sandwiches, apples, potato chips, string cheese, and snacks.

Faith noticed Finn always ate his dessert first. Today it was chocolate cake. She thought he was giving her a curious look. Maybe he could tell she had something on her mind, but she wasn't sure she should tell him or the others just what it was, especially after what had happened at her other school. This wasn't the first time she'd seen or experienced things others hadn't. What would the explorers think if she told them? Would they think she was crazy? What about the stick at the Hollows? Oliver and Finn had seen it.

Trusting anyone since her parents' divorce was difficult for Faith. She wanted to believe her new friends would understand what she wanted to tell them but then had images of them laughing at her. She decided she'd keep her secret to herself to be safe.

Faith watched the water in the creek as it gathered fallen leaves and then smoothly made its way around rocks. She thought, *This is the best place to spend the lunch hour.*

"Okay, Faith, what's up? You look pretty intense," Oliver prodded.

"Oh, it's nothing," she said, playing it down. "I forget to do an assignment. That's all. I'll just lose points until I make it up. No big deal. The world isn't coming to an end."

"Yeah, right," Finn said with a smile. "You're holding out on us."

Oliver said, "Look, Faith, you can trust us. Tell us."

"Let me finish my lunch. I need to think about it."

"Ah-ha, there was something," Finn declared.

"Finn, give her a break. She needs space with this," Dalton said.

"Okay, okay," Finn said with a feeling of defeat.

"Look, Faith, we'll respect your feelings about whatever is going on," Dalton said.

Things were quiet for a while except for the crunching of chips. From their spot they could see the forest. It was getting close to the first day of autumn. Spots of yellow and burgundy peeked through the evergreens. A slight wind blew across the treetops. Yellow leaves tumbled through the air and drifted to the ground.

Down at the far end of the field, football players chased each other trying to gain yardage. A kicker punted the ball high into the air, and it headed straight into the forest. A lone runner sprinted into the green, bushy entrance and disappeared. The others watched, awaiting his return.

Finn broke the silence. He always got antsy when it was too quiet, especially when things needed to be said. "Hey, I just thought of something. Dalton wasn't there yesterday. You know, the Hollows … the stick."

"What stick? What are you talking about?" Dalton asked. "You guys were at the Hollows?"

Oliver explained. "Finn and I were hanging out at Maple Park, and Faith came by on her way to the Hollows. We called you but your mom said you had a lot of homework to do."

"Right, I did. Tell me about the stick and the hollows."

Faith was quiet. Watching the forest, she waited for the football player to return with the ball.

Finn blurted, "It happened yesterday morning! We went to the Hollows and met up with some bullies. The same ones you see right now, down at the end of the field. They're always together. I know. I have to avoid them at all costs. They're the bullies who harass me about my glasses. I don't understand how you can play sports with them, Dalton."

Dalton explained, "You know, not all the guys on my team are bullies, maybe just a few."

"Well, yesterday I wasn't wearing my glasses. They didn't recognize me at all. It's like they don't see me as the person I am, a human being behind plastic and glass. They only see me as a pair of thick glasses. Anyway, as they came closer, I saw that it was Randy, Jarrod, Jeff, and, of course, their leader, Dustin, who asked where the pop bottle boy was, and then he tripped and went down face-first right into the ground. I looked to see what he tripped on and there on the ground was this big stick. I know it wasn't there before because we walked there. It just appeared out of nowhere. I'm sure of it. I would have tripped on it myself."

"A stick just appeared out of nowhere? Come on. Sticks don't just appear. It could have fallen down from a tree. Maybe the wind broke it off," Dalton rationalized.

Oliver explained. "No, this was from a deciduous tree. Probably a maple. And do you know what? There are no maples in that part of the forest. Those trees grow in other parts of the forest, on the hillside and on the far side of the school. Right there we have primarily coniferous. You know, they're the cone-bearing trees. They produce cones, like pine cones."

Dalton, still unconvinced, said, "Look, you guys. I have a dog, Keeper. I throw sticks to him all the time. Did you think about that? Maybe a dog carried it."

"Yep. We even thought of asking you if you'd been out there throwing sticks with Keeper. Funny thing though, we didn't see any bite marks. We determined the stick was definitely not there when we arrived. It was right in the opening. We all passed through that spot. Finn would have tripped over it for sure. He said so himself," Oliver recounted.

Faith finally spoke up. "Look, guys, let's admit it. Something or someone put it there to keep those guys from bullying us. Dustin's pretty tough, and he was so embarrassed he ran to get out of there. So something was definitely helping us."

Dalton was suddenly struck with what they were trying to tell him. "The apparition, the ghost from the night of the blue moon. You think he did it."

Oliver said, "You got it. Right now we have no other credible explanation, only the incredible explanation that this ghost or whatever it is seems to be on our side and is making himself known by sight and moving objects."

Even though she'd just recently met them Faith realized the boys were just like her. Maybe, just maybe, she wouldn't be so afraid to tell them what happened to her each time she walked into the school.

That night, Faith sat on her bed writing in her journal. She discovered that if she wrote about troubling issues, she could see them in a different light, sometimes solve them. Tonight she decided to write about trust.

Journal entry:

Today I thought about the idea of trusting. Can I trust these guys in the Explorers Club? What is trust anyway? I know I can trust Mom. Definitely. If I do something she doesn't like, I can trust that she'll ground me or take away some kind of thing that's important to me, like privileges. Maybe my Internet. Games. Moms are like that. You're supposed to be learning something from it. That's what they say.

Maybe there are different kinds of trust. Like, I can trust a best friend, if I had one, to keep a secret I tell her. Now if I tell my worst enemy a secret, then I guess I can trust that person would more than likely—yes, probably—tell others.

Okay, so maybe certain things can be said and certain things can't. The person you tell it to is important. Also, the people you're telling the secret to have to be respectful of you and deserving of your respect. You have to trust them never to do anything to hurt you.

I wonder if the guys in the Explorers Club would ever want to hurt me. I don't think so. I think they respect me. I think they deserve my respect. They're good people. They're not mean. Yes, I think I can trust them.

Tomorrow may just be the day I tell them about the school's front door. Maybe. Maybe I will just wait at the doors for them to arrive and walk through at the same time and see if something happens to them.

Yes. Good plan.

CHAPTER 7
The Door to the Hollows

FAITH STOOD UNDER THE BIG MAPLE TREE THAT OVERSHAD-
owed the school grounds just outside the offices. She was waiting for one of the Explorers Club members, curious to see if
he experienced anything unusual when walking through the
doors.

Dalton was rounding the corner about a block away, jogging
at a quick pace. He spotted Faith and changed direction to meet
up with her. "Funny seeing you here so early. I was just thinking
about you."

"Oh, and just exactly what were you thinking about me?"
Faith replied.

"Well, a few things, to be honest. One—how yesterday you
seemed preoccupied with something. It seemed to be something that really bothered you. Two—how you're a real positive
addition to our club and to the school."

"How so?"

"You're friendly, intelligent. You're easy to talk to. You're not preoccupied with the latest shows on TV, latest fashions, or gossip. I mean, in our club, we talk about science, exploring. You know just as much as we do. It's good to have you in the club. You know, most girls aren't interested in science or history."

"Thanks," she said. "I just don't care about all that other stuff." She kicked dirt with her sneaker. "I tried, though, but it didn't work. Then I'd be made fun of by the other girls just 'cuz I wasn't interested in what they were."

"Well," Dalton said, "it's good to have someone else in our club. Especially when they know as much as you do."

Faith's face turned red. She wanted to tell him about the door but was still afraid he'd think she was crazy and kick her out of the club.

"I have to get to basketball practice. You going in?"

"Yes," she said abruptly. Now was her chance to see if he got shocked when he walked through the door. She kept pace with him and barely brushed his shirt as they walked through the door. ZZZZZaaaap! Faith was knocked sideways. She turned and saw Dalton, who had a wide-eyed look, taking a step toward her. He reached out, grabbed her arm, and pulled her up before she hit the ground.

"What the heck was that?" Dalton asked. "Are you okay?"

"I think so. I'm pretty dizzy," Faith said. The green office door, the trophy case, and the big board with daily announcements spun around her like a carousel at an amusement park. She felt Dalton's grasp on her upper arm.

"Do you want to go into the office and sit down? Maybe they can help," he offered.

She tried to focus on the trophy case. "No!" she said sharply. "Take me to the bench just outside the gym."

They sat on the bench, and Dalton asked, "What the heck just happened?"

"Did you feel it too?" Faith asked.

Dalton's eyes widened. "I did! I don't know what it was, but it was powerful! Like something was pushing us." He looked around. "But no one was there."

Faith nodded in agreement.

Dalton looked at her. "Wait—this isn't the first time that's happened to you, is it?"

Faith couldn't believe it. It wasn't in her mind. She wasn't imagining things that weren't there. This was real. Not anxiety. Someone else had felt it too. This was definitely something real.

However, she wondered if she could trust him. Was he telling the truth? What she knew about him so far was that he was confident, open, and honest. *Okay, maybe I can trust him.*

So Faith took that leap. It was the first time since the divorce that she decided to trust someone. "Dalton … something has been happening when I walk through that front door. This thing, whatever it is, happens to me every morning."

"I've never felt it before, and I use that door every morning."

"I really want to talk to you about this, but you're going to miss your practice. Maybe we should talk at lunch."

"Should we tell Finn and Oliver?"

"I have a better idea," Faith said. "Tell you later."

"Okay, deal. I'd better run. See you at lunch. Same time. Same place."

"Got it."

Faith was elated. She no longer felt alone. Even more surprising, she'd written about this in her journal just last night. Was that a coincidence or what? she thought.

The rock, creek, and the giant log became the official meeting place for the Hollow Hills Explorers Club. Today they had to meet. Something was going on at Hollow Hills Middle School that couldn't be explained. It'd be during this lunch hour that they would decide how to move forward.

Dalton had his lunch and was heading over to the creek to meet up with the others when the football players shouted out to him, "Hey, Dalton!"

He changed direction and walked over to the ballplayers. After talking with them for a few minutes, he turned around and headed to the HHE meeting.

After getting her lunch from her locker, Faith had tried catching up with Dalton. She went down the hallway, out the door, and crossed through the courtyard but stopped when she saw him head over to the tough guys they'd encountered yesterday in the Hollows.

Instead of following Dalton, she sat at a picnic table, unpacked her lunch, and watched. She thought, *Is he good friends with them? How can he even talk to someone who bullies his own friends? I feel so bad for Finn, always having to watch out for them. I wonder if that's why he never buys his lunch. He probably avoids the lunch line where these guys might steal his money.*

She had just bitten into a peanut butter sandwich when three girls came over with their lunches. The one wearing a green-and–yellow striped top over blue jeans asked cheerily, "Hi, Faith, would you like some company?"

Faith was caught off guard. Her eyes were still glued to watching the football players, and her mouth was full of peanut butter. She looked up and tried to speak but her mouth was nearly immovable. "Uh … no … yes … I mean yes." She took a quick sip of grape juice from her juice box, swallowed, and continued. "I would like some company. Sorry, I don't remember your names. Obviously you know mine."

The three sat and the stripe-shirted one introduced their mini-squad. "I'm Callie, this is Sherry, and she's Mandy."

"Are you trying out for the cheerleading squad?" Callie asked.

"Tryouts are in two weeks and we're trying out. We've been practicing all summer!" Mandy announced.

"Yeah, you should give it a try," Sherry said as she opened a container of strawberry yogurt.

"Oh, I'm not so sure," Faith said as she hesitated eating her sandwich, not knowing whether the peanut butter would disable her mouth again. *How embarrassing*, she thought.

"Try out with us. We're awesome. We'll teach you," Callie said as she bit into her chocolate and caramel candy bar.

"Absolutely! We have two cheers and they're not hard at all," Mandy said as she reached into a bag of chips, fishing for those last tasty little bits.

"But like you said, you've been practicing all summer, so I'd only make you look bad," Faith replied.

"Understand something, Faith," Callie explained. "What we did this summer was plan the steps. We're just starting to practice. We have it all typed out. How 'bout we meet after school in the multipurpose room with the others who are trying out? Ms. Jinks is sponsoring the cheerleading squad this year. She'll be there to tell everyone what'll be happening during the next two weeks."

Faith liked Ms. Jinks, the science teacher. The idea of a science teacher leading the cheer squad made it all that more appealing. *It couldn't be all that bad*, she thought. *Maybe it'll be different at this school.*

"Well okay. I'll have to let my mom know I won't be home right after school. Make sure she didn't make other plans," Faith told them.

Faith thought, *I'm sure it'd be okay with Mom. But I really don't know anything about these girls. I'm not too sure I can trust them. What if they're setting me up? What if they're not? I'll never know if I don't try. I'll take a chance. Why not? I can always back out if I sense something.*

The trio of aspiring cheerleaders had turned into a quartet. While they ate their lunches, the girls talked about what they'd wear at the tryouts. They'd previously decided on the colors of raspberry, orange, and green and now would have to add a fourth color.

The bell rang, and Faith looked up from their little huddle and watched as Dalton, Finn, and Oliver stood and walked back from the creek.

She thought, *I should have told the girls I had to meet someone. I had promised Dalton this morning I would meet with them at lunch. I was the one who planned it. Talk about trust. They won't ever be able to trust me. What was I thinking? And me? A cheerleader?*

At the end of the day, the clanging of the final bell could be heard throughout the halls of Hollow Hills. Students filed out of classrooms in a race to go to lockers, catch buses, and go home; some would sit another five hours in front of computers doing homework and playing games. A few remained in the school for after-school clubs and teams. This afternoon, the school was hosting the first practice for those who wanted to become cheerleaders, and Faith had made up her mind to go. On her way to the multipurpose room, she heard someone calling her name.

"Faith! Wait up!" Dalton called as he strode to catch up to her. "Where were you at lunch? We waited for you. Remember, we were going to tell the others about what happened this morning, weren't we?"

"Yes, we were. Long story, but I'll make it short. I saw you going over to play football and then I was suddenly swooped up by three girls who invited me to try out for cheerleader with them," she hastily replied as she made her way down the hall.

"Hey, slow down there. I wasn't going to play football. They called me over to tell me they think I might be asked to play quarterback. Then I went over to eat with Finn and Oliver."

"Okay, my mistake. Where are you going now?"

"Football practice. How 'bout you?"

"Cheerleader tryout practice."

"How 'bout we meet after? Wait near the front door. You know, the bench there. I'll see if Oliver and Finn can hang around."

"Okay. See you. I really don't know why I'm doing this but Rah! Rah! Rah! Here I go!"

CHAPTER 8
The Ghost Takes a Walk

FAITH WALKED OUT OF CHEERLEADING PRACTICE AND IMME-diately felt the emptiness of the school. Most of the students were gone for the day.

However, at Hollow Hills Middle, there was a feeling of something more. It was as though an energy field was left behind, something you just couldn't put your finger on. Something that couldn't be seen, tasted, or felt but you sensed it was there. Like a bit of energy left behind that never dissipated when that final bell rang, a pulsing, electromagnetic wave surging through the vacant hallways.

Faith felt it as she left the cheerleading practice. She couldn't find the actual word to describe it, but she sensed it. Somehow she knew, deep in the hushed recesses of her mind, that something existed here in the hallways. She quickly flipped her head to look back toward the multipurpose room. Only a couple of would-be cheerleaders chatted away about jumps and choreography.

Faith turned to the right and found herself walking alone down the long corridor that led to her locker. She was sur-rounded by the black hole of after-school hallways. Her shoe was untied, and as she bent down to tie the fluorescent green laces, she felt a swift breeze waft through her hair. She tugged at her laces, tying them tighter for the walk home. As she did so, she looked down the corridor and caught a glimpse of a fig-ure turning the corner. *That's funny,* she thought, *I don't recall seeing anyone just a few seconds ago.*

She continued down the hallway, and when she came to the T-junction, she looked left: nothing. She looked right and still nothing. *Maybe,* she surmised, *it was the custodian, and he just slipped into his office.*

Faith continued to her locker without incident. She picked up her coat, put it on, and then began the long walk to the front door. She found Oliver and Finn sitting on the bench, totally immersed in their research.

"Hey, guys!" Faith said, breaking the silence.

The boys jumped at the sound of her voice.

"I didn't even hear you walk up," Finn blurted, trying to catch his breath. "How was practice?"

"What's wrong, Faith?" Oliver asked. "You look a bit pale, like you've just seen a ghost."

She looked around to see if anyone was coming. The three "sherbets" were down the hall within earshot, so she put her forefinger up to her lips. "Shhh," she said and then answered, "Cheerleading practice was fun. We learned the steps to the mandatory cheer. The science teacher is the host teacher. Isn't that interesting? A scientist leading cheers. I think she just might be my favorite teacher."

"When are tryouts?" Oliver asked.

"In two weeks. I have a lot of practicing to do."

"Show us what you've learned," Finn said.

"No way. Are you kidding?" Faith looked around and saw the trio nearing them. "Have you seen Dalton?"

"Not yet. He told us to meet him here. Have a seat. He'll be here soon," Oliver said.

The trio walked up to Faith.

Callie spoke first. "So what do you think, Faith. Have fun?"

Faith replied, "Yeah, it was fun. I have a lot of practicing to do."

"Hi, Finn. Hi, Oliver. Faith, we'll see you tomorrow," Mandy said as she kept walking with Sherry.

Callie called out to Mandy and Sherry, "Hey, wait up!"

Mandy and Sherry stopped and waited for Callie before going to the door. "See you, Faith," Sherry said.

The three girls reached the door, glanced back, and giggled before they pushed open the heavy green door and walked outside.

"What's got them so goofy?" Oliver asked.

Faith shrugged, not wanting to be bothered by their silliness. She said, "Listen, don't freak out by what I'm about to tell you."

"What?" Finn and Oliver said in unison.

"I think the ghost is in this school," she said quietly.

"No way!" Finn exclaimed.

Faith continued, "When I was walking to my locker, I thought I saw something down the hall. First, I felt a gust of wind blow through my hair. Then I looked up, and there it was, walking down the hall. It rounded the corner, and when I got there it was gone. Did either of you see anyone pass by just before I arrived?"

"No, I didn't hear or see anything, not even you. We were checking out investigative reports on ghost sightings," Oliver said matter-of-factly. "Are you saying that whatever it was passed by us?"

"Yes, it had to."

"Come on! Let's go find it. We'll search all halls and stairwells, see if anything appears," Finn said.

Just then the gym doors flew wide open and a loud raucous sound bellowed out.

Faith turned around to see the football players laughing as they exited the gym. She looked for Dalton in the group. He wasn't there.

A few more players walked by, and finally Dalton could be seen coming out of the gym alone. He walked to the group and said, "Sorry I'm late. The coach wanted to talk to me. Guess what! He told me he's made a decision and wants me to be the team's starting quarterback."

Finn said, "That's great. Congratulations!"

Oliver said, "Congratulations, Dalton. I knew you could do it."

Faith joined in, "Good for you! I'm happy for you! You must be really good. Quarterbacks have to be in top shape, run fast, able to think on their feet, and throw spirals. You know, before the divorce, my dad was teaching me how to throw one. It's really hard."

"I can help you out with that," Dalton offered.

Faith replied, "I'd like that."

Finn broke in, "Well, let's celebrate by finding ourselves a ghost."

Dalton looked at Finn and exclaimed, "A ghost?"

They explained the sighting to Dalton as they walked the halls searching for a ghost but discovered the custodian scrubbing black shoe marks from tiles and a math teacher sitting quietly in his room, popping chocolate-covered almonds and marking tests.

When they'd gone full circle, the four Explorers stood near the big green door in the foyer. Faith took a big, deep breath, filling her lungs, and as she exhaled she finally decided to tell the guys her secret.

"Stop, guys. I have something to tell you. Can I trust all of you? I mean, if I tell you something, you'll keep it a secret, right? And you'll believe me—whatever I say? I need your word," she said emphatically.

"Of course. Is this what you were going to tell us at lunch before you met up with the cheerleaders?" Dalton asked.

"Yes, it is," Faith replied. She took another deep breath, was quiet for a few seconds, and then continued. "Well, here goes. This morning and each morning since I started at this school, something strange has been happening when I enter." Faith pointed to the front doors. "Like a zap or a current of electricity poking me. It doesn't hurt or anything. It just kind of zaps me. And this morning, Dalton was with me when it happened."

"What about you, Dalton?" Oliver asked. "Did anything happen to you?"

"I felt something. It was something powerful and hard to explain," Dalton replied.

Finn said, "Maybe it's the security system. Maybe there's a short circuit. Do you touch the metal on the frame when you enter?"

With that idea they all walked over to the door and started their inspection.

"No electric eye here. No wires to be seen," Oliver said.

Finn began walking back and forth through the door to see if anything happened. "I don't feel anything. Why don't you try it, Faith?"

Dalton warned, "Wait just a second. What if she gets hurt? Faith, maybe you should just come in through another door."

Finn challenged him. "But how will we know the answer if she doesn't try it? I mean we're all here to help if something happens."

Faith said, "I don't mind going through it. I've been doing it every day since I registered."

Dalton replied, "Maybe we should have the custodian look at it."

Finn added, "And while we're at it, we'll ask him to help us hunt for the ghost of Hollow Hills Middle School. Right."

Faith said, "Okay, I'm going through."

Dalton caught her before she reached the door. "How about if I go with you at the same time like we did this morning?"

Oliver said, "Wait. Let's do this right. Dalton, if you go with her at the same time, you have to be shoulder to shoulder. No, that won't work being how you're taller. I know what. Just make sure you're touching at some point. You see, I do believe electricity is involved, and if a current's going through her, you'll be connected and the current will continue through you when it goes to the other side."

Dalton and Faith stood in front of the door ready to walk out when Oliver yelled out, "Hey, wait! Faith, you said it happens when you arrive in the morning, right? What happens when you leave at night?"

Faith replied, "I haven't noticed. It's always so crowded at the door. So I guess nothing happens that I've noticed."

Oliver continued, "Okay, so walk through to the outside and come back in side by side, touching at some point."

So they did. Dalton, Faith, Oliver, and Finn all walked outside together. They dropped their backpacks on top of the dirt mound that surrounded the base of the big maple in front of the school.

Dalton and Faith went up to the door and took their places, standing side by side. Dalton took Faith's hand and they walked toward the door. Dalton reached out, grabbed the metal handle of the green door, and pulled. Nothing happened. He pulled again. Nothing.

"It's locked," he said.

Faith tried the handle. Nothing.

Oliver spoke up. "Uh, guys. We forgot one thing. After hours, the doors are locked. You can go out from inside but you can't get back in."

Finn exclaimed, "Oh no! I should have known that! I forget my homework all the time and have to return to the school. It happens a lot. Then I have to find which room the custodian is cleaning. Sometimes if its real late, I walk around the outside of the building and look for a room with lights on. That's usually where he is. Then I knock on the windows and he'll unlock a door and let me in. He kind of expects me on a regular basis. I think the real reason I forget my homework is because I have an unconscious desire not to have to do all that busy work. But my mom always makes me go back to school and get it."

Finn walked to the door and knocked loudly. "Maybe we can get him to open it for us now. Wait, wait, wait, bad idea. It only brings us back to having to explain to him that only one of us feels a zap and we're wondering if it's from the ghost that's walking around the halls."

Oliver said, "You're right. We'd look pretty stupid. Okay, so we have to modify our plan a bit. Everything stays the same except for the time. We'll do the experiment when the doors are unlocked. What time in the morning does the custodian unlock the doors?"

"I know they're open by at least seven thirty because I've had practices that early," Dalton said.

Faith said, "I had to meet with the counselor before school to get my schedule and it was seven forty-five. Oh, by the way, I had mentioned to her that I felt odd when I entered the door and she chalked it up to a bit of anxiety, you know, nervous about my first day at my new school. But I'm not so sure. I don't feel nervous anymore and it keeps happening."

Oliver modified the time. He was actually typing the entire experiment on his notebook. He said, "Okay, so I have us starting at seven forty-five just to be safe. We'll all meet here at seven thirty and make sure it's not crowded at the door when we begin. At that time there shouldn't be too many students here. Buses usually begin arriving at eight o'clock. Okay, does that sound good to everyone? We meet right here at the old maple at seven thirty?"

All agreed. It was a good plan. They took one last look at the door before leaving. As Faith started to turn around, she saw him. It was out of the corner of her eye, but she saw him. He was in the stairwell looking out through the window.

"Look, there he is."

The boys turned around. The ghost disappeared.

"Where!"

"He's gone now. He was looking out the stairwell window."

"Come on, let's go inside. I'll go find the custodian," Finn said.

"No, I have to get home; it's getting dark," Faith said.

"Me too. We'll meet tomorrow and see what happens," Dalton said.

Oliver added, "Remember, we begin promptly at seven forty-five."

CHAPTER 9
The Other Side

It was 7:20 a.m. Faith was early. She was excited about today. *What's going to happen at exactly 7:45 a.m.? Will it happen to the others?* she wondered.

Faith loved fall with its crisp morning air. A soft breeze blew, picking up a crimson leaf, carrying it through the air and laying it gently a few feet from the front door. She felt a chill and zipped up her jacket. She walked to the sidewalk and looked down the street. She could just barely make out one figure walking toward the school.

A movement in the school caught her attention. She looked through the big green door and saw someone walking down the hallway. He was pushing a large cart. It must be the custodian.

The breeze gusted. Faith looked up and saw that the nearly bare branches of the maple looked skeletal against the gray sky. It was 7:25. She heard the faint sound of voices coming from down the street. She spotted all three of her new friends walking together.

Oliver was already making notes. He said, "Glad you're here early, Faith. Since we're all here, let's push the time up. So whenever you're ready."

Finn said, "Ready to get zapped, Dalton?"

Dalton responded, "Absolutely. How 'bout you, Faith?"

"Ready," she answered.

Oliver said, "Okay, at 7:35 a.m., you go through. So let's prepare. We want to make sure no one else enters at the same time. Just the two of you. Finn, keep a lookout."

Finn reported, "Okay, coast is clear on both sides of the walk. Wait! Here comes a car and it's pulling into the staff parking lot. It's Ms. Redding. We'll have to wait."

As Ms. Redding, the librarian, walked past, she looked at the group with eyes that could drill right through you. That look was usually accompanied by a big *sssshhhhhhhh!*

In unison, the Explorers Club said, "Good Morning, Ms. Redding," sounding like a guilty gang of cookie robbers.

Ms. Redding drilled them with her eagle eyes and said with a sharp bite, "Why are you students here so early? What are you up to?"

Oliver spoke first. "We're here early so we can go over our homework together. We want to make sure we're doing everything right."

Ms. Redding, with a touch of skepticism coloring her tone of voice, said to the group, "Well in that case, you're welcome to use the library."

Oliver replied, "That's very kind of you. We'll be in momentarily."

Ms. Redding gave them one last look, turned, opened the door, and entered the school.

Finn watched through the windows on the side of the door and saw Ms. Redding as she rounded the corner. He said "Phew, that was a close one. Okay, coast is clear. Let's get ready to do some zapping!"

Finn kept a watch from the sidewalk. Dalton and Faith walked to the door with Oliver close on their heels. When they were two feet from the door, they stopped.

Looking at Dalton, Faith said, "Okay, ready when you are."

Dalton took Faith's hand, and when he moved his right foot, Faith moved her right foot. Then a step with their left. Only one step away.

"Go for it!" Oliver exclaimed.

After that command, with their right foot first, they both stepped across the doorway and followed with their left. After a sharp blue flash of light and a loud pop, everything went dark.

Finn and Oliver had to close their eyes. A few seconds later, the two squinted, trying to focus on the door. However, no amount of focusing would help these two boys see their friends because Dalton and Faith were gone. They had vanished!

"We did it. We did it!" Dalton exclaimed.

"You got zapped too?" Faith said.

"Oh, yeah! It happened. Oliver, write it down. It worked!"

Oliver didn't respond.

"Oliver! Finn! It worked!"

Still no response.

"Where are they? I don't see them," Oliver said.

In amazement, Faith said, "They can't see us!"

Oliver and Finn stood there for a few minutes, not moving an inch.

"That was way too cool!" Finn cried out. "They must be inside the school. Let's go."

Faith and Dalton watched as Oliver and Finn walked through the big green door, stopped, and looked left, down the hallway, and right down the other.

Oliver looked at Finn and Finn looked at Oliver and in unison they cried, "They've disappeared!"

Oliver said, "Wait a second. The librarian. Of course, they went to the library."

Dalton said to Faith, "Follow them. They're headed to the library."

When Finn and Oliver walked past old "Eagle Eyes," she said, "Good to see you, boys. Where did your other two friends go?"

They had to think quickly. What could they say? Finn thought of something. "Oh, they disappeared down the hallway. Probably needed to check something out."

"Take a seat at one of the tables and keep your voices down to 'inside voice' level," she instructed.

Finn and Oliver walked over to the far table. From this vantage point, they could see through the windows that ran across two of the library walls. More teachers arrived, making a beeline to the staffroom, desperate for a morning cup of coffee before continuing down the hall to their respective classrooms.

No sign of the missing. Hallways had filled with early morning club-goers. Finn and Oliver were becoming more worried by the moment. Oliver had his notebook open. He checked his notes in hopes he'd see something that would tell him just what might have caused the disappearance. Then, like so many of his other bright firefly ideas that seemed to light up in his mind, he had a brilliant one.

Oliver excitedly exclaimed, "Finn, they completed the circuit! You see? Here, I'll draw it out for you. Here's the doorway. When Faith went through alone, she would just get zapped, but when the two of them went through, Oliver touched his side of the door frame and Faith the other side. Could it be that if the current of electromagnetic waves was actually strong enough they wouldn't even have to touch the frame? It would just be able to circulate through them as long as they were close to the wave."

Finn replied, "But that doesn't exactly explain the missing zappers."

Oliver whispered, "No, but they must be somewhere, and where that somewhere is, I don't know. They're made up of energy, and energy doesn't just disappear, it goes somewhere. We just have to determine where that somewhere is."

Faith and Dalton caught up with the two boys inside the library. Faith tapped each on the shoulder. No response. She brushed Finn's hair. Nothing. Again.

This time Finn felt a tickle on his head. He raised his hand and smoothed down his hair.

Faith did it again.

He felt it again and said, "Must be a spider." This time he put his head upside down, shook it, and quickly brushed both hands back and forth through his hair.

"Do the hair thing with Finn one more time," Dalton said.

Faith gently brushed her hand through Finn's hair.

Finn shook his head back and forth and then turned his head upside down and shook it again, fiercely rubbing his hands over and over his scalp and jumping up and down.

Dalton and Faith watched as the librarian came over and said in a quiet voice, "Young man, you obviously have a serious problem with your head. I suggest you go to the office and have the nurse check you for bugs." She turned and walked over to a nearby shelf.

"Dalton, I can't believe this. I think we've completely disappeared. They have no idea we're here. What if we can never return?" Faith asked, feeling a sense of desperation.

Dalton said, "Let me see if this will work. See the pencil Oliver's using? I'm going to see if I can make it fly out of his hand." He gently touched the pencil. There was no reaction.

Oliver began swizzling the pencil between his thumb and forefinger. Dalton tried it again, and this time he took hold of the eraser end of the pencil, yanked it from Oliver's grasp, and flipped it high into the air. It flew end over end toward the ceiling, soaring across the library and finally coming down with a plunk on the table right next to the librarian's work area.

The librarian abruptly poked her head around the book shelf, marched over, and snapped it up.

"Did you see that?" Oliver asked.

"Yes, I did. So did someone else. Uh oh. Here she comes, the eagle-eyed gatekeeper. How did you do that?" Finn whispered in his quietest "inside voice."

"I didn't do anything," Oliver whispered.

Ms. Redding, with determination, plunked the pencil in the center of their table and snapped, "Boys, I must remind you to keep your voices down, and no fooling around."

"Uh-oh." Dalton watched the librarian reprimand Oliver and Finn.

"Sorry, it was a mistake. The pencil must have slipped. Won't happen again," Oliver reassured her.

"This is getting scary. Be careful. We could get them into serious trouble if we don't watch out," Faith cautioned.

The librarian turned on her heels and proceeded back to her desk like a soldier watching over her village.

"I think it might be a good idea to leave and see if we can find them outside. They're going to be late for class," Oliver said.

The bell rang with a loud, continuous clang.

Finn exclaimed, "I'm outta here."

Oliver said, "Me too. Wait up."

The two gathered their books and papers and rushed shoulder to shoulder to the door, plowing into it at the very same time. Wham! They were stuck in the doorway, struggling like a couple of bear cubs caught between two rocks!

With a fierce look about her, Eagle Eyes started marching to the door but was headed off as Dalton rushed right through her and gave the two boys a hefty push. They went tumbling, freed from the grasp of the library. Both looked back to see if the librarian was the guilty party, if she had literally booted them out. Not a chance! She hadn't even made it near the doorway.

Finn and Oliver reached their lockers, assembled their belongings and ran to class and to their desks. They sat down and looked at each other with that shared look of knowing that something unbelievable had just happened!

Faith and Dalton ran after them and walked into the classroom.

Finn mouthed the words, "Something weird is going on."

Oliver nodded.

On the way to their seats, Faith and Dalton poked the other two a couple of times.

Finn and Oliver looked at the two empty seats ahead of them, felt a slight poke on their shoulders, turned around, and eyeballed the students sitting directly behind.

"What? What'd I do?" the innocents cried out.

Finn looked over at Oliver, who was shaking his head.

Oliver whispered, "What's going on?"

The teacher began taking attendance and said, "Dalton."

Dalton said, "Here!"

The teacher repeated, "Dalton."

Once again Dalton said, "Here!"

Faith's name was called. "Faith."

"Here!"

"Faith."

"Here!"

The teacher asked, "Has anyone seen Dalton or Faith?"

No one answered.

Oliver volunteered to take the absentee sheet to the office.

Dalton looked at Faith, nodding his head toward the door. Both stood up and followed Oliver as he left the room, looked up and down the hallways, turned, and walked into the office.

Dalton nudged Faith and nodded at a boy who was coming toward them. The boy was walking slow, his hands in the pockets of brown slacks. He had on high-top leather boots and his brown jacket was worn.

Faith saw him. She was thinking that something about him was so familiar yet very different. She couldn't remember ever having seen him before, but something about him kept tugging at her.

Just then, a girl with red curly hair came bounding out of a classroom, but instead of passing by the boy, she went right through him. Faith and Dalton gasped. Then the boy stopped and stared directly at them as the girl passed right through them and disappeared into the office.

The three stood looking at each other with wide-eyed stares.

Then it hit Faith like a hard ball thrown to a first baseman. She knew who he was. She knew where she'd seen him. It was at the Hollows on the night of the blue moon.

He was the apparition in the forest and the apparition in the hallway and the stairwell.

CHAPTER 10

Lunchtime Plan

"TOMORROW WE'LL BEGIN A NEW SECTION ON THE SUBJECT OF probabilities. Who can tell me what the word 'probability' means?" Ms. Billiards, the math teacher, asked.

Oliver thought that if someone disappears in a flash, there's a great probability the person's in a parallel world.

"It means something is likely or will probably happen," Dalton answered as he walked into the classroom followed by Faith. They both walked up to the front of the classroom and placed their late slips on the corner of Ms. Billiard's desk.

"Sorry," Faith said.

"Hope it won't happen again, but there is a small probability it might," Dalton said with a big grin.

As Faith turned around, she saw Finn and Oliver were scowling, as if asking—*What happened?*

Dalton mouthed, "Later."

Dalton and Faith sat only seconds before the bell clanged. The four rushed to be the first through the door. They had a ten minute break to exchange information. It wasn't enough time to tell Oliver and Finn about the experience they had.

"Are you okay? What happened?" Oliver asked as they walked down the hallway to their next class.

Finn, walking backward and facing the other three, said, "Yeah, you two created quite a spectacular zap before your disappearing act. Where'd you go?"

Dalton was the first to answer. "Look, we're going to keep it simple as we have only nine minutes left. First, after going through the zapper we found ourselves still in the lobby. Second, we could see everyone and everything and we could hear everything just as before. Third—and this is the biggie!—no one could see or hear us. And fourth, everyone walked right through us."

Oliver opened his notebook and began taking notes as he walked. He said, "So you were invisible to us but you could see us. What about touch?"

"After a couple of times, I could make your hair move," Faith said.

"So that was you—my hair, the bugs. Did you also have something to do with the pencil soaring into the air?" Finn asked.

"No, that wasn't me," Faith said as she giggled and pointed at Dalton, who was laughing.

Finn gave Dalton a shove.

"Now wait, you guys, there's one more very, very important thing. Fact five: Dalton and I saw the boy from the Hollows.

Right here in the hallways. We even talked with him," Faith added.

The Explorers froze. Total silence. This was big. This meant the two had gone to another place, a place that existed at the very same time as their own existence. They stood there in a circle like they were in a world of their own, looking from one to another with eyes as big as an owl's.

"Another dimension," they all said at precisely the same time.

Students passed by the Explorers, some with scowls, others with a look of curiosity. Some even purposely bumped into them without an apology.

It was Oliver's voice that broke the silence like the bell that clanged through the halls, announcing they'd better break the huddle and get to science class. "Meet for lunch by the creek. Our plan is for all of us to go together through the green door."

The four were the last to go through the classroom door. Just in time. Ms. Jinks was just coming from her lab, the little prep room that connected two science classes. She wore her white lab coat and carried a jar of pond water. She took attendance. Everyone was present.

Ms. Jinks started the lesson for the day by asking, "Have you ever tripped and fallen into a puddle of water or dipped your hand into the ponds out by the Hollows? There's an amazing world of life you do not see, but just because you don't see it with the naked eye doesn't mean it doesn't exist."

Dalton, Faith, Finn, and Oliver all looked at each other, smiling.

Ms. Jinks went on. "Today we're going to look through our microscopes to explore and discover that amazing life. In your

science journals, you'll make field notes on everything you discover, including that which the microscope enables you to see as
well as things you can't see with just the naked eye. Please make
use of your artistic abilities and draw what you see, and record
descriptions such as shapes and sizes, like circular, spiral, flat,
long, narrow, wide. Does it move? And how does it move? Or
does it remain still?"

Someone in the class moaned, "Ooooooooh."

Another said, "I'm not touching it."

Ms. Jinks commented, "Don't worry, it's nothing you hav-
en't touched before. Just be sure to wash your hands afterward.
Many of you will view the world a bit differently after today's
class. Now get into your groups and begin by having one of your
members join me here at the sink to collect your sample of pond
water. The rest of you begin by preparing your microscopes."

As the group of four huddled around their microscope
viewing their sample of pond water, Dalton commented, "Yes,
Ms. Jinks sure is right. When you see things that you usually
can't see, it sure does change your view of the world."

Oliver added, "Is this a coincidence or what?"

"Tell us about your plan," Finn impatiently demanded.

Faith said, "Okay, so after we eat lunch we should have
enough time to attempt entry through the door as a group of
four, all touching."

Finn remarked, "Yeah, right. That's going to look a bit odd,
don't you think?"

Faith said, "We have to do it when nobody's looking. We
don't have to be holding hands. We just have to touch. So we
can be side by side, two by two."

All four agreed that when they go through the door, the ones positioned side by side were to touch hands in the middle, and the two in the back would put their outside hands on the shoulders of the two in front.

"Still, it's going to look very odd if someone happens to notice," Oliver commented.

"You know what's going to look even stranger? The four of us getting zapped and disappearing!" Finn said, chuckling.

"That's why it's so important that nobody's around when we do it," Faith said emphatically.

Finn said, "We could ring the fire drill. Everyone will be going out the back doors and behind the school. We'd have all the time in the world to go through the door."

Oliver said, "No, we wouldn't. The fire department gets here pretty quick and uses the front door. Plus it'd be wrong. Did you know if they find out who did it, your parents have to pay a fine? No, it's wrong and definitely not worth it.

"Okay, so we just keep an eye out for a break in the hall traffic. Best time would be ten minutes after the bell rings. Everyone's pretty much settled into the cafeteria or wherever they're going to eat. If we wait too long, students begin walking around the halls with their cliques, plus there's too much traffic to and from the office and library," Oliver said.

"Good points. Okay. There are a couple of benches in the front foyer, so what do you say we eat our lunches there while you two tell us about the apparition. We can watch for a break in traffic all at the same time," Finn suggested.

Everyone agreed. It was a good plan.

"We'd better get down to business here. Ms. Jinks just started her rounds. Let's see what we can discover in this pond water," Dalton said.

The Explorers set out to see what their naked eyes couldn't.

The bell rang announcing lunch. Everyone hurried to clean up their area. Final notes were written and handed in. The group of four left for their next experiment: their lunchtime experiment.

Fortunately, the benches in the front foyer were free, and the group settled in like they were making camp in the field where they would soon discover the undiscovered.

Faith ate her egg-salad sandwich and kept an eye on the east wing hallway. Dalton had a roast beef and cheese sandwich and was in charge of watching the west wing. Oliver ate a cucumber sandwich and watched the hallway to the cafeteria, and finally, Finn enjoyed a piece of German chocolate cake and then a thick peanut butter and banana sandwich. He watched traffic coming out through the office doors. No one could witness this. This was exclusively for the HHEs.

It was quiet save for the sound of munching and crunching. Their concentration was intense. The HHEs could almost feel any slight movement the others made. The air felt electrified.

About eight minutes into lunch, Finn exclaimed in a garbled voice all rich with chocolate, peanut butter, and banana, "*Now!*"

And with that, the four jumped from their seats, Dalton opened the doors. They all walked outside, assembled side by side directly in front and back of each other, placed their hands in the agreed-upon manner, and walked swiftly through the door.

Zzzzzzzzap! Yellow lights, purple lights, blue, green and orange lights flashed before their eyes. Deafening thunder crashed all around them. They had done it! All four of the Hollow Hills Explorers exclusive club had passed through the zapping doorway.

They looked around. It was like nothing had happened. Everything was the same. In the office, the secretaries were working, teachers were chatting with one another. Down the hall, two students exited the cafeteria and walked to their lockers. Others entered the gymnasium for noon activities.

"Everyone okay?" Faith asked.

All heads nodded.

"All right, let's walk around. Keep a lookout for our forest friend," Faith instructed.

Still stunned, Finn asked, "Who?"

"The apparition in the Hollows. Remember? This morning when Faith and I entered through the door we actually talked with him," Dalton explained.

Finn replied, still a bit stunned. "Oh, yeah."

Just then the office door opened and Principal Towers burst out. She was on another one of her missions with her black heels pounding on the floor sounding like a big bass drum, chin sticking out, fiery red hair pulled to the back of her head into a tight little bun and tied with what looked like a black pirate's flag. This mission was bringing her on a collision course with the four.

Finn muttered, "Uh oh, we're in trouble now. She's moving like a tank and heading straight for us."

Dalton said in a muffled voice, "Don't move. Wait and see what happens."

The tank in the tight black skirt plowed right through the four Explorers and moved straight down the hallway.

"Unbelievable! Did you feel that?" Oliver exclaimed.

"Like a tornado blasted through me! I feel sorry for the one she's after."

"Okay, let's look around. We'd better hurry."

The four began their lunchtime exploration by visiting the cafeteria. They walked from table to table saying hi to students they knew. No one replied.

Finn pointed to Jeff, Dustin, Randy, and Jarrod, the boys who were always bullying him. "Let's go over there and see if they see me."

The four walked with caution over to their table.

Finn said, "Hey there!"

They didn't respond.

Finn, with newfound confidence, sat next to one of the them. "Hey, guys, I'm here. Aren't you going to bully me? Look, look at my glasses."

The boys didn't move. They didn't even look at him.

Finn placed his hand above Dustin's head and pulled on a few strands of hair. Dustin brushed his hand through his hair.

Finn said, "Wouldn't it be cool if I could touch Jarrod's pizza and slide it down the table?"

Dalton said, "Not so sure that'd be a good idea."

Finn reached out and hovered his hand over the pizza, and just then Jarrod grabbed his slice of pepperoni pizza and took a humongous bite.

Dalton ordered Finn, "Come on, Finn, you're just stooping to their level. It's not like you to bully someone."

Finn said, "How 'bout just one orange? It'd roll like a bowling ball right into those juice boxes. Strike!"

Dalton pulled him away and they left the cafeteria.

They passed students in the hallways and walked right through some of them and then headed to the multipurpose room. They looked inside and spotted the three sherbets practicing their cheer.

Faith exclaimed, "Hey, they're practicing. Why didn't they ask me to practice with them?"

"Maybe they couldn't find you," Dalton said.

"Let's watch for a bit so I don't fall too far behind. Over there—let's sit on that mat." Faith pointed to a spot on the far side of the room. They all walked around the three cheerleader hopefuls and sat.

"Okay, let's try it again. Ready, go!" Callie directed.

"One, two, three, four, five, six, seven, eight. Two, two, three, four," they counted as they moved across the floor.

"No," Callie said. "I walk forward and you two walk back four steps and then we come back together."

Mandy said, "It'd look a lot better if we had four people. It would even it out."

"Well, that isn't going to happen," Callie replied emphatically, tossing her head and whipping her ponytail to the side. I told you why I wanted Faith to come and learn that other cheer with us."

Callie continued, "Now here's the plan. Just before tryouts we tell her we've decided to use our old cheer. We'll apologize and tell her she can't do it with us because she doesn't know it. That way she'll have to go out there by herself and use that cheer we've been teaching her. Little does she know we didn't make it up. It's from last year's dance squad. They made it up. When she tries out with it, the judges will chase her right out of the gym. Everyone'll hear about it—that she copied it and tried passing it off as her own.

"She's going to look bad, sooooo bad, and I don't mean bad in a good way. Then Dalton won't even give her the time of day and we, future Hollow Hills cheerleaders, will have a chance with him."

Dalton's jaw dropped and his face turned bright red. The other Explorers looked at him. Faith's eyes grew bigger as she looked back at the sherbets.

Mandy replied, "Okay, okay. I get it. I get it. But hear me out a second. What you plan to do could really hurt her. It just isn't nice."

Callie ordered, "Well aren't you a Miss Nicey Nice? If you're not interested in becoming a cheerleader, you can leave now, otherwise let's get to work."

Faith knew her tears were coming and knew Dalton was watching her. She ran out of the multipurpose room and down the hall. She heard the boys yelling for her as they followed. She cut across the courtyard and the field, heading straight to the creek, where she sat on one of the big rocks.

The boys arrived seconds later.

Dalton asked her, "You okay?"

"No, not really. I thought I could trust them. They seemed so excited about having me in their group. I mean … well …

I'm new here and I thought people here were so much nicer. It's no different from my last school. The same thing happened. Why do people like to do mean things like that? Why would they want to do that to me? I haven't done anything to them. I was nice to them."

"Didn't you hear them?" Oliver asked. "They think Dalton likes you and they want you to look stupid to him. They're trying to set you up!"

Faith repeated, "But I trusted them. How can I ever trust anyone after this?"

Oliver interrupted her before she ran any further with the pity party. "Look, Faith, you can trust some people to be your friend and support you, and some people you can trust that, if given the chance, they'll stab you in the back.

"Like 'flavor of the week' cliques. One week they kick a girl out and talk about her behind her back. The following week she's back in and another girl's out. Well, you can trust that this week you're out and maybe next week you'll be in. That's trusting them for who they are and what they'll do as the flavor of the week clique."

Dalton added, "You have to decide if you want to be part of that."

Faith asked, "Well, what about you guys? How can I trust you?"

Dalton said, "You can. I mean—you've gotten to know us a bit. You're not a threat to us. And we're not like that anyway. We've been pretty open and honest with you. Trust me, and I mean, well, we wouldn't need or want to do anything to hurt you."

Finn said, "This is all interesting, this trust thing, but what's she going to do about cheerleader tryouts?"

Faith said, "That's definitely not going to happen."

Oliver stopped her. "Wait, wait, wait a moment. Faith, you have a choice here. You can choose to let them defeat you, or you can choose to come out of this looking good."

"What are you talking about, Oliver?"

Oliver, the logical and level-headed one, explained. "Okay, listen up, I think I have a plan. Let's say you go along with their plan. You go to the practices and pretend to learn their cheer but secretly at home you make up a cheer they don't know about, and when they spring their underhanded plan, you just go ahead and try out with your own cheer."

"Alone?" she asked.

"Alone and on top! It's how you look at it. It's one way of handling their bullying. It's like when you're sailing and the wind blows harder and harder—by this I mean the bullies—and you pull tighter and tighter on the sail trying to control your boat. If you keep pulling, you'll keel over," Oliver said. "The best thing to do is take your sail down, out of the wind, and the wind—the bullies—will keep blowing and it won't even bother you. So some things you'll just have to do alone. Don't fight them, question them, or do anything to them. Just pretend to go along with it and then do your own thing."

"Mmmm—interesting. I'm kind of looking at this in a different way. Kind of from the other side. Things don't look so bad now," she said.

"Can you make up your own cheer?" Dalton asked.

"I'll give it a try. I just might be able to handle this. I can use this as an opportunity to stand up and not fall down when girls play their tricks on me. I want to be taken seriously. I really want to be respected in my new school."

"Hey! Look! I see it. I see it. It's him!" Finn exclaimed.

"That's him all right. Calm down, Finn. We don't want to scare him away," Faith said.

"Scare him? He's the ghost. He's supposed to be scaring us away!" Finn shot back.

Faith responded, "I think you'll see that he's a bit different than the typical ghost."

The four Explorers walked toward the ghost. Finn and Oliver, not knowing what would happen, slowly walked behind Faith and Dalton.

"Hey there, Dalton. I see you've brought more friends with you, Faith," the ghost said.

"Hi, Tom," Faith said. "These are my friends Oliver and Finn. Guys, I'd like you to meet Tom."

"Uh, hi," the boys said.

Faith could see in their expression that they couldn't believe they were being introduced to a ghost. "It's okay, guys."

"I'm not gonna hurt you," Tom added.

"Have you always been able to walk around inside the school?" Finn asked.

"If you're askin', 'Is that principal gonna gimme the boot?,' the answer's nope. She can't see me. Never been able to see me. I've been here longer'n she has. I know I look younger'n Principal Towers and don't really know how that works. Just kind'a stay in my teens. I watched this school being built and I've been here ever since it opened and no principal's ever been able to ketch me," Tom said, chuckling.

"Has anyone else been able to see you?" Oliver asked.

"Once this wise ol' man, and most recent this lady—l'il lady, with long black hair, lives in a cabin far up the mountain there. One night when the moon was full, a real harvest moon, golden as the leaves of the maple that time of year, the time of year when the days are as long as the nights, you know when farmers start harvestin' the final plantin', fillin' their root cellars with what all they canned or preserved. Well, this li'l lady, she showed up in about the same place where that front door to the school sits. At first she was frightened right outta her socks, but I calmed her down real quick like when I told her who I was and how I got here. We walked over to the Hollows and sat and talked for a spell as that harvest moon made its way 'cross the sky," Tom said.

Oliver asked, "How long have you been here? I mean, have you always been a ghost?"

Tom answered, "Oh, no. I came here shortly after the lumbermen set up camp just through the forest there in what you call the Hollows. I was about fifteen, a bit young, when I came to work here with my pa. One day a terrible storm blew itself in real fast and then it all happened. I's just 'bout ready to drive my axe into a cedar and a lightnin' bolt, well it hit me and there was a bright blue flash and darn if a fire didn't spread itself through the forest and next thing you know, I was walkin' around in the forest feelin' like, well, like I's hit by lightnin'. The worst part was no one could hear or see me. I guess that's when I became what you call a ghost. The forests were all burnt up and all the lumbermen musta run and headed out, so you can imagine how happy I was when the old man and then the li'l lady appeared."

Oliver said, "You mean to say the lady appeared when there was a full moon."

Tom answered, "Yep, and she comes back often, always seems to be near a full moon."

Oliver said, "I wonder if the full moon has something to do with our being able to cross over. But then it was a blue moon, which doesn't happen often."

Tom answered Oliver's thesis. "I think what happens is that when the blue moon appears, the li'l lady's able to visit, but when the next full moon comes, she stops visitin' for a while."

Oliver said abruptly, "That's it. The blue moon must open the door, which is available until the next full moon at which time it closes—let's say, the gate."

Tom answered, "Yep, you might have something there. So I'll be able to visit with you for just shy of one month. Sounds good to me."

Faith said, "So that explains why the door becomes electrified—if that's the right word. Just before the blue moon when I walked through it, I got zapped. After the blue moon, I was able to step through, and that's when I saw you."

Finn had a question. "What about the others in the school? Are they able to come through?"

Just then the clang of the bell rang through the hallways. Students began coming in from outside, flooding the hallways, heading toward Tom and the group of four. The floodwater of students rushed closer and closer, passing right through the small group, one after another as if the group didn't even exist—at least in the same dimension.

"Come on, let's go. We're going to be late! Finn exclaimed.

"Head toward the front door," Dalton directed.

"Wait, wait, wait! Tom, I want to find out more. Can we meet this Friday night so I can take notes? I need to explore this before the next full moon," Oliver begged as he closed his notebook.

"Yep, I'll see you then. There's a lot you might wanna know about this area and things that happen that you can't see," Tom said.

"Hurry up, Oliver; if you don't come with Faith, you might not be able to make it through," Dalton said.

"Okay, okay. I'm coming. I'm coming," Oliver snapped. Just then he had an idea. "Hey, do you think Tom could ever come through on our side? Say if he were in contact with Faith?"

"Let's talk about that later. Right now we have to get through the door. We don't even know if we can. We've never even tried. We're winging this whole thing. Hurry!" Dalton yelled.

The Explorers came running around the bend and spotted Principal Towers standing in the foyer watching for hall runners. She stood with her heels planted shoulder width apart like a sturdy, powerful basketball player setting up a block. She was immovable. She stared straight ahead, watching and waiting.

The four knew they had to exit the school first before getting into position for reentry. There was no time to dally. They ran at the door and right through Principal Towers, who lost her balance, spun around, wavered, and attempted to regain her stance and composure. Once she did, she plumped her hair, retied her pirate's flag to her bun, took her blocking stance, and once again glared down the hallway like a laser gun ready to blast foreign invaders.

Principal Towers said, "I definitely have to cut back on that coffee!"

The HHEs positioned themselves on the other side of the door, making sure of their contact with one another.

"Ready?" Faith asked.

"Ready," their hurried reply came.

"Then let's go!" Faith announced.

There was a moment of bright light filled with all colors of the spectrum, ranging from deep violet to light yellow, along with flashes of white light. Then the four fell forward toward the door and were so absolutely close, within a fraction of an inch, of taking out the principal.

Dalton, quick on his feet, pushed the others to the side as they gained their balance and hurried around the principal.

She sharply remarked, "Pushing it a bit late, aren't you? You'll lose your privileges to go home for lunch if it happens again."

They looked at each other, trying to stifle a laugh, and then headed onward.

Later that evening, Faith sat on her bed and wrote in her journal about the events of the day. She was still trying to make sense of it all.

She wrote:

Today the other Explorers went through the door with me. It worked. They got to meet Tom. We're going to meet again this weekend.

Something really bad happened. It's just like my last school. This group of three girls who wanted me to try out for cheerleader were really planning for me to look like a fool. They plan on dropping me from their group just before tryouts.

Dad, you said it would be better for me in the country. I guess it is; you were right, except the girls in the school aren't very nice, at least the ones I've met, but I think I can handle them.

You haven't been to see me yet. I know you said it would be better if we wait until Christmas, but I think you're wrong. I know it's a long ways away, but maybe you could stay in a motel that's close by or something. Christmas is too far away. I don't think I can wait that long to see you. If things don't go right at cheerleader tryouts like I have planned, I just might find a way to take the bus to come stay with you because I don't want to be at a school if it turns out like the last one. So be watching at the bus stop for me. I wish you could read this. I love you.

Faith put her diary back in its secret spot inside the old carved-out book. As she drifted off to sleep, she thought about trust. She knew she could trust her mom, but at Christmastime she would be with her dad, and she could trust him to be there.

Faith knew she absolutely could not trust the sherbet gang. Well, she could trust them to be mean to her.

But best of all, she had three new friends she knew she could trust to be her friends. She was thankful for the Hollow Hills Explorers Club.

CHAPTER 11
Faith Kicks It Up

HERE WAS FAITH FOR THE FIRST TIME IN HER LIFE, DECIDING she no longer wanted to be a loser. She wanted to be strong and stand up. She wasn't going to be the brunt of others' jokes. She'd devised a plan. She wasn't too sure of the outcome, didn't know if it would work or fail, but she was going to do it. Not just try but actually do it.

As she walked alone from her locker, down the long hallway to the girl's changing room, she held her head high, her heart beating nearly as fast as the wings of a hummingbird. She was going to meet up with the three sherbets. She knew their plan. She knew they wanted her to look the fool. She was going to go along with their plan—up to a point.

This time Faith decided to take fate into her own hands. She picked herself up, held her head high, and walked into the changing room to face whatever they felt they had to do.

The sherbets were on the far side of the changing room all dressed in colors that clashed with what Faith was going to wear. They sported pastel colors of lime green, raspberry red, and bright orange. True to spirit, they wore the shortest skirts Faith had ever seen, topped off with a tight striped T-shirt matching the skirts. Faith didn't have anything to match this. This had to be part of their plan. Truth be told, these girls played really dirty.

"How do you like our new outfits, Faith?" Callie asked.

"They're ... uh ... cute, but ... uh ... I wasn't aware of any change from the purple and blue we chose the other day," Faith said, playing along.

"Oh, I guess you weren't aware ... uh ... of course you don't know. Sorry," Callie said in a syrupy-sounding whine. "We forgot to tell you. Uh oh. We changed our cheer and could only work it out for three. We're doing it in a V formation, and so you understand, a V formation can only be done if we have three, so we couldn't work you in. Don't get me wrong—we tried as hard as we could, but we just couldn't make it work—but don't you worry—you will look good doing the required 'success' cheer. You'll do just fine. We'll be rooting for you!" Callie finished off in a singsong voice as she turned and tugged on her skirt.

Faith stood there seemingly in a trance. She knew of their plan, but part of her couldn't believe they would follow through with such a cruel thing. But they had and she had to accept it. She had to hold it together. She bit her quivering lip. Her eyes welled with tears. She blinked back the wetness. Whispering voices could be heard coming from other girls in the changing room. Faith heard gasps and then more whispering. She slowly looked around. Girls held their hands over their mouths. Some looked away.

Faith watched as the three sherbets stood in their cheer pose with their hands on their hips wearing confident smiles, looking like they held the school in the palm of their hands. She also saw the way Callie was looking at her, at Faith's shaky knees, the tears in her eyes. Callie could barely hide how happy she was to have ruined Faith—or at least attempted to ruin Faith.

Something else was happening, though, and Faith sensed it. The other two sherbets stood alongside Callie, but the look on their faces wasn't quite the same as Callie's. In fact, they looked sorrowful as they edged away from Callie and tried to face the other way.

Faith thought, *Could it be they may be thinking twice about trying out with Callie? They keep looking at me with that sorrowful look. Now they're moving away from Callie. They must see that what Callie's doing isn't nice.*

Mandy and Sherry slowly turned away and looked at each other. Mandy raised her eyebrows and Sherry bit her lip. Both turned slightly and saw their reflections in the mirror. Mandy smoothed her hair and Sherry smoothed her lipstick.

Callie turned toward the exit and pranced out and into the gym. The door closed. The other two looked at each other, and Faith thought for a moment they weren't going to follow Callie. Mandy shrugged. Sherry nodded in the direction of the door. The two pushed the door open and reluctantly walked into the gym to join Callie.

Faith stood in the changing room feeling alone and in shock. They did it. It was real. Taking a deep breath, she walked to her locker, changed her clothes, and brushed her hair. She began to feel a strength rising in her body. She knew she had to put her plan into gear. She'd practiced all week. Last night she'd played this entire scene out in her mind's eye. She knew what to do. Now or never!

The others watched Faith as she walked out the door and into the gym to face the judges and all others to prove to them and to herself that she could stand up to anything they threw at her.

The cheerleader candidates sat on the bleachers behind the table of six judges consisting of Ms. Jinks, the science teacher; Mrs. Towers, the principal; Mr. Arpel, the music teacher; Mr. Lawrence, the band teacher; Mr. Davies, the boys' wrestling coach; and Sandy Matthews, last year's head cheerleader.

Ms. Jinks stood, turned around, and faced the girls. "Okay, ladies, today you're here to try out for the squad of cheerleaders. We have ten spots this year, as we plan to attend the competitions hosted by the National Cheerleader Association."

The girls all cheered, clapped their hands ecstatically, and stomped their feet on the bleachers, making a rumble like thunder that grew louder and louder.

Ms. Jinks raised her arm high above her head, signaling silence and waiting for the noise to subside, and then once again addressed the crowd. "Each group's name has been written on a card and dropped into this hat. We'll be pulling your names at random. One group will be waiting on deck as the other tries out. Please be as quiet as possible until your names are called. Are there any questions?"

None. Only tension and fear in the gym. You could just feel it. Hearts were beating rapidly as adrenaline pumped through their fit bodies.

The tryouts began. Ms. Jinks called the first group. "Gazelles are up first. Blue Dolphins—on deck."

The Gazelles performed a cheer that included a three-person pyramid. It was lively and executed with enthusiasm. The crowd clapped and cheered.

The Blue Dolphins performed a cheer that was mostly movement similar to a drill team. It was filled with lots of staccato beats. The girls' kicks, turns, and jumps were in time, not missing a beat.

Ms. Jinks called one group after another. As they finished the girls relaxed, but those who were still to be called became more nervous by the minute. Faith was in the latter group. She was running her routine through her head over and over. She knew her name would be called with the Cheetahs (the group she referred to as the sherbets), and she knew they would inform the judges that she wasn't in their group anymore. Faith was sure they would do it in a way to make her look bad, but she was prepared for that too.

Two groups were left. Girls kept glancing in Faith's direction, wondering what she would do. Ms. Jinks called the next group to go on deck. It wasn't the Cheetahs. That meant they were to go last.

Finally, the time had come. Ms. Jinks stood and surveyed the neon and pastel colored crowd of hopefuls. She announced, "Next on deck will be the Cheetahs—Callie, Sherry, Mandy, and Faith." The girls stood. Callie walked up to the judges and announced, "I'm sorry to inform you, but Faith is no longer in our group." She looked directly at Faith and added, "Her choice." Then Callie turned and pranced over to be with the Cheetahs.

Ms. Jinks walked back to Faith and quietly asked, "Is that correct, Faith? Your choice?"

Faith looked up to Ms. Jinks and said, "I really didn't have a choice. I just found out in the changing room."

Ms. Jinks asked, "Are you comfortable with this decision? Because I can insist you try out as a group."

Faith said, "Ms. Jinx, I think I'll be okay. Thank you for your concern."

Ms. Jinks walked back to the judging table and the tryouts continued. The White Clouds did an excellent job. This competition was tough. These girls were good.

Now it was time for the Cheetahs to go. They walked up, formed a V just as planned. Callie was in the center with Sherry and Mandy on the sides.

Faith walked up to stand on deck.

Callie called out "One ... two ... three ... four ... ready. Hit it!" and they were off and running. They were well practiced with kicks, jumps, and side passes. Sherry and Mandy crossed back and forth. Callie timed it just right and ran forward and back, weaving between the other two.

Now it was time for the famous pyramid. Sherry and Mandy got down on their hands and knees side by side. Callie executed a split jump behind the girls and then placed one foot on Sherry's back and one on Mandy's with perfect timing. She stood, straightened up, felt the balance, and then raised her hands and arms high in a big V. But the V began leaning sideways, like the Leaning Tower of Pisa. Then Mandy collapsed into Sherry, and Callie fell backward, landing on her backside with both legs in a big V stretching straight up into the air.

The Cheetahs scurried off, trying to ignore the crowd's encouraging clap, which was not quite as loud as the clap for other groups. Callie sat down, giving the other two members of her group a blaming look accompanied by a sneer and click of her tongue.

Faith stood on deck, her heart beating so hard she thought it would beat right out of her chest. "I can do this, I can," she affirmed herself.

"Faith is next. Please ready yourself." At this very moment Faith began to put her plan into action. At home, she had connected her computer to her keyboard, and then she and Oliver recorded a background of rhythmic drumming and chanting. Yes she was alone, but not completely. She walked up to the music teacher, Mr. Arpel, and gave him Oliver's notebook, which was all prepared. All the teacher had to do was press the space bar on the keyboard when Faith nodded to him. Faith ran to the center of the gym, turned around, and smiled at the crowd.

All eyes were on her. The gym was so silent, you could have heard a ghost tiptoe across the floor. There was movement behind the windows in the doors at the back of the gym. *Oh, no*, she thought. Three sets of eyes trying to watch the tryouts. Three sets of eyes that belonged to Oliver, Finn, and Dalton. Faith looked up at the bleachers. There he was, sitting in the far corner, top row. It was him. Tom. He gave a nod, as if to say, "Go for it, you're ready."

Faith looked back at the group, smiled, and nodded to the music teacher. The sound of drumming could be heard as Faith started out with a rhythmic stamping of her feet and clapping on the offbeat. She kicked her leg high, nearly touching her head with her foot. The crowd gasped and clapped. Faith did a few short steps to the right, a split jump high into the air, and then ran to the left side and did the same jump. The entire time she yelled out a chant no one had ever heard. Totally original! The crowd was listening. This was new and it was good! Then Faith combined dance and cheer steps, moving in a circle, heading away from the judges' table. The crowd was so moved by the music, chants, and Faith's choreography that they began clapping with the beat.

Faith was now in the center of the gym, facing the crowd. She ran five steps forward and did a round off into a back handspring, ending in a split. The crowd yelled and clapped loudly. They all stood up whistling and stomping. Except one. Callie sat in her spot on the bleachers surrounded by the stomping herd of girls. She clicked her tongue, rolled her eyes, and finally stood up, clapping her hands two times.

Faith couldn't believe it. It worked. She had faced her fears and the bullies' plan and she had come out on top. The girls had applauded her. For once she felt accepted. She no longer felt alone. She looked up to see the top bleacher empty. Tom was gone.

In the back of the gym, the three guys all trying to see through the little window must have accidentally pushed the handle because the door popped open and the three tumbled in, falling on top of each other. The crowd turned around to see the boys spread out on the floor. The three stood, red faced, mouthing, "Sorry, sorry," walking backward until they felt the door behind them. They turned and ran out the door and down the hall.

Ms. Jinks tried to speak over the laughter. It slowly subsided. "Okay, girls. Now you'll all be doing the required cheer together. You'll be forming one line across the gym. Please find your spot."

The girls quickly ran to find a spot. Most chose to stand next to members of their own group.

Ms. Jinks directed, "Starting at this end"—and she pointed to the right—"count off in threes."

The girls counted off one, two, three, one, two, three until they reached the end of the line. Then Ms. Jinks surprisingly separated the girls by asking, "All ones step forward five steps. All twos step back five steps. All threes step back fifteen steps. Now put your hands and arms out and make sure you have your own space and won't accidentally kick someone in front of you or behind."

Ms. Jinks made a few adjustments to the lineups, and she announced, "Now you'll be doing the required cheer a number of times, and after each time, we'll have the front line go to the back and the middle line will move up, and then the same with row three until you've all had a chance to be in the front and the judges are satisfied they've been able to see each one of you. Is everyone ready? Okay, here we go. I'll count you off. One, two, ready, go!"

All thirty-two girls were off and flying through the difficult steps choreographed for the tryouts. The competition was tough. The girls were practiced. Faith kept up with the girls to her side. She was smiling now with confidence. One might say she was beaming like a ray of sun shining through a break in the clouds. She was trying hard not to look at the window at the back of the gym for fear she might laugh. She had to focus her concentration on the cheer.

After each line had come to the front and judges were satisfied they were able to observe all girls doing the required cheer, Ms. Jinks rose and said, "Girls, I'd like you to thank the judges for giving their time to helping us with the tryouts. Let's give them a hand."

The girls all clapped, jumped up and down, and kicked their legs, trying to emulate Faith's kick.

Then Ms. Jinx said, "Girls, all of you have done a wonderful job. It'll be very difficult choosing a group of only ten. The results for this year's cheerleader squad will be posted outside the office window by eight tomorrow morning. Those chosen must attend a noon meeting on Friday. Please bring your lunch."

As they left, girls crowded around Faith, telling her she did an amazing job. They all wanted to know where she learned to dance and cheer like that. She thanked them for the compliments and said maybe she'd let them know tomorrow.

She didn't go to the changing room. Instead, she went to the rear gym door to meet up with her friends.

"Where did you learn to do what you did in there?" Finn asked.

She told them the same. "Maybe tomorrow," she said. "But you know what? I did it. I had a plan and it worked. I didn't let them put me down. So until tomorrow ..."

And they all headed down the hallway. Following behind them wearing a big smile was their new friend, Tom.

That night she wrote in her journal.

Today I found out about real trust. I found the most important trust you can have is in yourself. I took the risk and trusted that I could do it and succeed and I did it. I just had to trust myself. I guess it's about confidence too. By trusting in myself, I gained confidence.

I'm really thankful for the support of my new friends, all of them.

Dad, I guess I can wait until Christmas to see you. I won't be catching the bus tonight.

CHAPTER 12

Friday Night at the Hollows

ON FRIDAY NIGHT THE FOOTBALL BLEACHERS WERE FILLED with cheering crowds. Hollow Hills had just won their first game of the district tournament that was to continue through the evening and all day Saturday.

Dalton took off his helmet and headed for the locker room to shower. He had plans, and they didn't include watching the next football game.

In the hallway he met up with the other members of the Explorers Club. They walked to the front door, walked outside, turned around, and lined up, shoulder to shoulder, two by two. They were fortunate the doors were unlocked for the tournament.

Oliver said, "Everyone ready?"

"Ready," Faith said.

"Ready," Finn replied.

"Let's go," Dalton directed.

Once again they held on to each other, step by step, and—*zzzzaaap!*—once again, a brilliant light blinded their sight. It was followed by a booming and deafening sound.

When their vision and hearing settled, they realized something wasn't right. They were no longer in the school. They were in the middle of a forest, quiet and still.

"Wow! Where are we? What happened to the school?" Oliver asked.

Dalton replied, "I don't know. I don't recognize a thing."

Faith was startled. "Did we do something wrong?"

Oliver added, "Wrong? How do we know what's wrong or right? We're totally new to this type of exploration. I think we've entered another world."

Finn said excitedly, "Wait, guys. We're not lost because we're always somewhere, and I always bring my GPS with me. I'll find out just exactly where we are." He took the device out of his backpack, pressed a few buttons, and in no time at all announced the precise latitude and longitude readings in exact degrees and minutes. Then he declared, "I know where we are! According to this, we're at the same location as the front door of the school."

A voice came from behind them. "Ya got that right," Tom said. The ghostly apparition walked up to them, appearing as a white hazy figure and then slowly developed into a solid teenager with honey-colored hair. He wore a red-and-blue-checked flannel jacket and brown trousers with suspenders. "Relax; you're right near the logger's camp. That's my axe you see there sittin' in the stump. Now you remember where that is, right? Follow me. I'll take you to that place you call the Hollows."

They all followed, crossing through a dense forest blanketed with fern and soft moss. The smell of campfire smoke wafted past their noses. Soon they arrived at the loggers' camp. Canvas tents housing the loggers were propped up and scattered along the hillside. Some glowed with amber light from the setting sun, casting a palette of oranges and yellows against the hillside.

The group stepped quietly until coming to a spot that had previously been logged. As they walked into the center, they recognized it to be the Hollows. Fresh notches on stumps filled the air with the scent of cedar. A fire pit in the center sent a steady stream of smoke as hot embers slowly extinguished. Tom stirred the embers, and they glowed with a brilliant reddish orange. He added a few thin sticks that quickly caught fire. Then he placed small logs with care in a pyramid-like fashion.

The five sat on cut logs surrounding the growing fire. Bright orange flames licked at the air. The five felt the warmth and sat hypnotized by the fiery shapes formed while Tom added more logs.

"It's good to have company here who knows what happened after the lightning struck and that wildfire wiped out the forest," Tom said.

"So the loggers here can see you?" Oliver asked as he typed precise notes into his notebook.

"Yep. What's happened is, you've landed in a different time. I'm not sure they can see you, but they'd probably be shocked if they did. They've never been able to see the li'l lady who lives on the mountainside."

Finn said, "If we landed in another time, how can satellites triangulate and give me coordinates if they don't exist in that time? Wait! What if they're able to send and pick up signals across time or dimensions?"

"Good observation, Finn," Oliver said.

"Will we be able to get back?" Faith asked. "The green school door's gone."

"That's right. 'Member the axe in the old log I told you to watch out for?"

"Yeah, the one we saw when we entered? The one where the door used to be?" Finn asked.

Tom replied, "Yep, that's the one. You see, I's working on that log there when the lightnin' struck. It must've hit me, the axe, and the tree. Then when the lightnin' hit, the forest and the fires started up. Well, it wiped out most of this forest here, which was primarily cedar. Years later it was taken over by redwood. When that got logged or burnt down, alder and maple came along in parts of the forest. I've watched it all. But my axe, and the petrified log it's wedged into, have always been there."

Oliver surmised, "I think I know what's happening. The electrical charge must not have been able to ground itself into the earth. Maybe the charge just keeps circulating and never dissipates."

Tom continued, "So when you leave, you'll all have to touch the axe, and you should be able to go back."

Faith said, "What I don't understand is why I was able to see you in the halls and others couldn't. I also don't understand why I'm the only one who feels the charge at the front door if I go by myself. The others don't feel it unless we make contact."

Tom replied, "I can't answer that except maybe you have some kind of connection to the area. I don't know. Can't tell ya."

Dalton suggested, "This just might be an interesting project for Oliver to research."

Oliver added, "Let me ask the first question. Could it be that you're more sensitive to electromagnetic waves? Has anything strange like this ever happened to you before, Faith?"

She slowly looked away from the fire, trying to hide anything they might recognize as a yes. She thought, *I just might be able to trust these guys with a bit more.*

"Ah ha! Do I detect a smile? Are you hiding something?" Dalton asked. "I'd also like to know how you learned to dance like you did at cheerleader tryouts. Congratulations, by the way. You'll make a great cheerleader."

Faith, welcoming the change of subject, replied, "Thank you, and about the dance ... well, at my old school, I started hanging out with a bad crowd and got into a lot of trouble. And I do mean a lot. So I had to make a choice, and I finally chose not to hang out with them anymore. I didn't need the hassle, plus my parents started their divorce and I had to find something to do. It was getting pretty harsh. I had a lot of alone time and found the Dance Place just around the corner, so I started hanging out there after school. It was really good for me, a fun place with positive people. I helped out with straightening up and keeping the floors clean, and they taught me to dance."

"Okay, that explains the dance. Now how about the door?" Finn insisted.

"I really don't know about the door. What I can tell you is that strange things have happened to me before. Strange things I can't explain. Maybe we can make them our future projects and you guys can help me to figure them out. That's enough for now, guys. Maybe we'll talk about it the next time the moon is full. Now, how about we sit here for a while and appreciate the warm fire and good friends?"